"How do we survive?" someone shouted from behind where Benny stood.

"Some of you won't," the man said bluntly. "But many will, enough to rebuild a wonderful culture and society and preserve much of what is already there. Your job is to save the old art and culture and build new on top of it."

Suddenly, beside Benny the professor shouted out, "We won't remember any of this, will we?"

The officer smiled. "It is possible, but unlikely," he said. "Most of you won't remember any of this."

That stunned everyone even more than the death sentence he had just declared on many people in the room.

Benny smiled at Gina and pretended to tip his hat at her in thanks.

She smiled back and nodded.

"I wish each and every one of you luck," the man said. "The future of the human race on the planet Earth depends on all of you."

THE HIGH EDGE

THE HIGH EDGE

ALSO BY DEAN WESLEY SMITH

THE HIGH EDGE

A SEEDERS UNIVERSE NOVEL

DEAN WESLEY SMITH

wmg
PUBLISHING

The High Edge
Copyright © 2022 by Dean Wesley Smith
Published in a different form in *Smith's Monthly #11*, August, 2014
Published by WMG Publishing
Cover and Layout copyright © 2022 by WMG Publishing
Cover design by Allyson Longueira / WMG Publishing
Cover art copyright © Philcold
ISBN-13: 978-1-56146-729-7
ISBN-10: 1-56146-729-4

For Kris

THE DISASTER

CHAPTER 1

Somehow Benny Slade survived almost everyone else in the world dying.

One minute he went into his old steel vault that filled the back room at Benny's Personal Loans to get some cash for his next loan and when he came out, both Madge and Maggie, his two right hands, were laying face down on his newly installed brown carpet in the front office.

Madge, who looked more like his old mother used to look before she got hit by that cab, had fallen next to her always-neat and clean desk while Maggie, about two years younger than Benny's twenty-eight years, had sprawled in the middle of the floor, her short skirt riding up and showing him a little of those wonderful white panties of hers that he liked so much.

He had just come out of the vault with the two hundred and sixty in cash for Mrs. Tenny's loan. He dropped the money on his desk and just acted, not thinking.

First he called out to Maggie and kneeled beside her and checked her first. He couldn't find a pulse and she wasn't breathing.

Then he jumped over beside Madge. Same thing.

No pulse, no breathing.

Both were dead.

He sat back on his heels, still beside Madge.

He could feel that cold, hard feeling coming over him like it did when he had been in a firefight in Iraq.

He hadn't felt that in four long years.

He had hoped he would never feel it again.

With that cold, hard feeling, emotions got shoved back. He had needed that to happen in the gulf and it happened now.

He just stared at the two bodies in front of him.

What had happened? No one had come in or out because the bell hadn't rung on the door. And he had only been in the vault for less than thirty seconds.

It took him a good twenty seconds of staring at his two dead friends to figure out what was different, what was wrong besides two healthy women being suddenly dead.

He just kept kneeling there, staring until he finally saw it.

There was no blood.

Nothing.

They just lay face up, eyes wide open, completely dead.

"Move, Benny," he said out loud. That finally got himself into motion.

He stood and went to the phone and called 911, staring at the two women on the floor while he waited.

But no one answered.

With the phone to his ear, he went back and checked both of them again.

Very dead.

Very.

The phone was still ringing at the emergency center.

What had happened?

His first thought was gas attack, which got him moving even faster.

He took the phone and scrambled back into the vault.

He had left the vault door slightly open when he came out, so if it was some sort of terrorist gas attack, he was as good as dead as well.

Besides, he had stayed out in that front office for a good minute staring at his two friends and trying to call for help.

After fifteen seconds of standing in the dark working slowly to control his breathing, he got disgusted at himself.

"Come on, Benny, get it together. Do a little thinking. Use your damn head."

Madge had always complained he talked to himself too much, but Maggie thought it cute.

Maggie had thought anything he did cute, and he had thought she was cute.

They had flirted since the first day he hired her six months before. She was as sharp as they came and knew money and books and computers, even though she hadn't finished more than a year of high school. He was attracted but had managed to keep the relationship on only flirt level.

She had been fun, just not his type.

Even though he came across as the military type, he had

two degrees from the City University of New York, including one in math. He liked women to be much, much smarter than Maggie. But she had still been fun to flirt with.

He went back out and stared at the two women on the floor. The phone to the emergency center was still ringing.

He hung it up and tried again.

It just kept ringing.

911 was slow at times in New York, but not that slow.

He didn't hang it up, just sat it on the desk and stared at Maggie there on the carpet for a moment. He was going to miss those white panties she flashed at him all day.

He was also going to miss her laugh and her smile and that wonderful blonde hair.

The coldness inside him whelmed upwards and he pushed those thoughts away. As his sergeant used to say, "Time to fight, time to think later if you survive the fight."

His sergeants over the years, all of them, had always been annoyed that he thought too much and didn't react quick enough when needed.

Clearly, this was some sort of strange fight he was in. He needed to get moving.

He turned away from Maggie and headed for the door.

At first, he opened the door slowly, not sure what to expect.

The moment the door cracked open, the wave of sound hit him like a hammer. He hadn't noticed that before because he always just blocked out any sounds from a New York street. Anyone living in the city needed that ability or otherwise go stark raving crazy.

He opened the door completely and stepped outside, going down the four small steps to the sidewalk.

The day was comfortable for an early summer day, with high overcast clouds that threatened rain. It wasn't very warm at all and wasn't supposed to turn hot for over a week. He hadn't been looking forward to the heat because he normally wore jeans, a long-sleeved shirt, and a sports coat over his shirt. Today he had on a tan shirt and dark-brown sports jacket.

But when the city turned into a giant sweat-box, he couldn't dress the way he liked and that just irked him.

He stood and took a deep breath of the cool afternoon air. Then he made himself really look at what was around him.

Up and down the street and on all the side streets hundreds and hundreds of car alarms and sirens were all going off at the same time.

Drivers were still in their cars, either slumped over, or head rolled to one side, held up by their seat belts. Cars had piled into intersections, had smashed into parked cars, or run up and against buildings.

Most car engines were still running, some racing as if their occupant still had a foot on the gas. Up Lexington Avenue he could see a fire starting to take hold of a building.

But what he didn't hear through all the noise were police and ambulance sirens.

And no one around him in the cars or on the sidewalk was moving.

No one.

This was some bad shit. Of that he had no doubt.

He quickly checked a couple of young girls on the sidewalk

near his office front door to be sure they were dead. One had on a short blue skirt that had ridden up when she fell to show no underwear and he covered her up before checking her.

They were as gone as Madge and Maggie, eyes open.

He stared at their faces. They had not died in pain, that much he could tell.

No wonder no one had answered his call at the emergency number. From the looks of this, they were dead as well.

Then, up the street, he saw some movement as people came up out of the subway and sort of stopped and stared.

"So I'm not the only one," he said, feeling fantastically relieved.

He started toward the other people, then saw a couple of them panic and flee back down into the subway, followed by the others.

"Won't help," he shouted. But no one was going to hear anything over the noise of the car alarms and engines.

But they were doing exactly as he had done when he ran back into his old vault.

He glanced around at the buildings towering over the canyon of Lexington Ave. He couldn't see one window opening, or anyone even peaking out at all the noise.

And as far as he could see in both directions, everything was stopped and bodies covered the sidewalks.

He walked up to the corner of 54th, carefully walking around the bodies. He looked both directions.

Same thing along the tree-lined street.

Everyone was dead, knocked down by some sort of giant killer in an instant.

From what he could tell, not a one knew what hit them. None of them looked shocked or panicked or were showing any fear at all.

Just normal expressions on very dead people.

"What happened?" he asked out loud, but the words barely made it to his own ears in the noise of alarms and running cars.

Who knew that the end of the world was going to be so damned loud.

"I need to find out how far this spreads," he said into the noise.

He could feel the panic he had learned to hold down when he was a kid in fights on the street and when in the Iraq war start to ease up into his gut. He hadn't felt that in many years. It wasn't the dead bodies that bothered him.

He had seen worse.

Much worse.

Dead bodies after the first few months in Iraq had stopped bothering him, at least on the surface. His counselor at the VA said he had a lot of buried anger and that the only way to get healthy was to let out some of the anger and tell the counselor what he had seen.

He didn't want to tell anyone, so he and counselor hadn't gotten too far in the last few years.

Death didn't really scare Benny, but there were dead bodies on his street, in his own business, and he was still alive.

Now that scared hell out of him.

He started to head back to lock up his vault, then laughed and looked around. Unless this was the second coming and everyone was going to suddenly spring back to life, locking up his money was the least of his worries.

But he went in and locked the vault anyway, tossing the money back inside that he had taken out to loan Mrs. Tenny for her grandkid's operation. More than likely Mrs. Tenny and her grandkid weren't going to be needing much of anything anymore.

CHAPTER 2

"What a mess," Gina Helm said, her voice soft, the shock she was feeling making her voice a whisper that didn't carry very far in the almost empty banquet room.

The hotel-like banquet room was large enough to hold five hundred people, but only she and ten others were in the room, staring at a large screen on the wall. Some were almost not breathing, a few were covering their mouths and crying silently.

The image panned over the area of the planet below where in ten days they would rescue the survivors from that last deadly pulse of electromagnetic energy from an exploding neighboring star. The images they were getting were from about five hundred feet in the air. The bodies of the dead littered the ground seemingly everywhere along the streets of one of the planet's largest cities.

In places, a few people moved among the bodies, but mostly all she could see was a sea of death.

How was a disaster like this even possible? The scope of it just stunned her.

She covered her mouth because she wanted to be sick, finally making herself turn away from the images of the dead for a moment. She strode for a few paces in the large, empty room, trying to clear her mind a little.

She was the tallest in the group at six foot, so her strides were long and covered distance across the hard, tan-carpeted floor. She had very short, black hair and she kept herself in perfect shape. Her steps were almost silent. She had on white tennis shoes, jeans, and a long-sleeved white blouse with the sleeves rolled up.

Her normal working clothes.

Today was not a normal working day.

She didn't like the feeling of being sick, of feeling helpless in any situation. She had learned to always be in top shape and never feel helpless on her home planet a few hundred years before, when as a young woman she had needed to become a survivor.

And she had.

Now she was here to try to help the survivors below.

She needed to pull herself together.

She turned and instead of looking at the large screen panning over the streets of death, she just stared out the huge wall of viewport that covered one side of the big room.

The beautiful planet drifted below, whites and blues swirling over the large oceans. It seemed so calm and peaceful and reminded her a lot of her home world. Looking at the planet through the wall-sized viewport, you could never tell the billions of humans who had thrived on that beautiful planet were now dead. Only a few million survivors remained.

She forced herself to take a few deep breaths to calm herself.

There were almost a thousand humans on this huge space-ship called *Star Conscious* that now orbited the planet. The crew and people like her on board were from over four hundred planets in three different galaxies near the Milky Way. Her home planet was in the Lesser Maganelic cluster of stars.

Everyone on this ship was a Seeder, part of an ancient organization of humans that seeded human culture on all Earth-like planets and then helped the human cultures survive and mature.

The planet below had been seeded.

She had been recruited to be a Seeder off her home world when she was twenty-five and now a few hundred years later she still looked the same, since once a person became a Seeder, all aging and disease was cured from the body.

The Milky Way had been completely seeded and the front edge of the Seeders had moved on to the Andromeda Galaxy and its surrounding satellite galaxies before she had become a Seeder. She had joined in with the social services branch and in two hundred years had been embedded on nine different worlds at different levels of development to help move the culture of that planet forward.

The planet below had been seeded in the third sector, so it was in the early space-age period of growth, one of the most dangerous periods for any culture. Only the humans on the planet below would now have to start over and build again.

She had no idea how long it would take them to get back to where they had been in development. Or if they ever would.

The mission below would be her tenth, and so far the most challenging. She had no idea how to help survivors just live and start to rebuild a civilization taken from them without warning in an instant.

The Seeders, even with all their ships and skills, hadn't been able to do anything to help rescue the billions of humans on the planet below from instant death, but they could rescue and help the survivors.

The *Star Conscious* had just arrived in orbit less than ten minutes ago, right after the first big death pulse. If that pulse would have been allowed to hit this ship, some inside would have died as well.

The Seeders who had been embedded on the planet below had escaped on one ship and would be returning to also help with the survivors.

Helping the survivors was why she was here. She and at least a thousand others covering the planet were going to help the survivors move forward as fast as possible, start to rebuild over the next twenty or thirty years.

But first they had to rescue as many as they could of the survivors from a second coming disaster. This planet wasn't going to be struck with just one electromagnetic deadly pulse, but two, the second one coming in just ten days.

Right now, from another more advanced part of the Milky Way Galaxy, ships were speeding here to try to pull off the planet the almost two million survivors and move them out of harm's way when the second huge pulse washed over the planet.

Then they would put everyone back to start the rebuilding process.

All of those ships from the Milky Way Sector One had Seeders embedded secretly in the crews. Every planet eventually discovered that they had been seeded at a distant time in their past, but the common knowledge was that the Seeders were long gone. In reality, Seeders were everywhere, secretly helping every culture advance and survive. Only the main wave of Seeder ships had moved on out of the Milky Way.

This ship was only one of four completely Seeder-run ships on this rescue mission.

She looked around. The large room looked like it could hold a banquet with a hundred tables. It had lights recessed in the ceiling and tan walls. In ten days this room would be full of at least three hundred survivors from below.

And thousands and thousands of other rooms like it on this ship and a thousand other ships would be full as well.

Staring out at the beautiful blue planet below, she just hoped enough of the other ships would make it in time to save every survivor from the second pulse.

CHAPTER 3

Benny headed downtown along Lexington, stepping over and around the dead bodies on the sidewalks. He thought these sidewalks used to be crowded when people were alive. When the same people were sprawled all over the place, not moving, the sidewalks got even smaller.

A number of places he had had to walk out in the street to get around cars smashed up on the sidewalk. And in two places he had to actually climb over the hood of a car to even get up the street.

Most everyone had either their business clothes on, or summer clothes, so there was a lot of skin showing.

A lot of very dead skin.

He kept staring up at the buildings around him, looking for movement in any window.

Nothing.

Thank heavens the day hadn't turned hot.

Down a dozen blocks, he saw a few more people gathered near the entrance of the subway, looking terrified and very panicked, but at least this group had gotten over the desire to flee back into the tunnels. More than likely this was their second time to the surface.

Benny crossed the street, giving them a friendly wave as he went toward them. "Anyone have any idea what happened?"

All four of them, including a nice-looking young thing with blonde hair and a light blue backpack over her shoulder, shook their heads no.

One guy held up his cell phone. He looked to be about five years older than Benny and had more hair than any guy should ever wear in his mid-thirties. It was tied back into a ponytail.

"Phones are working, but no one is answering anything," he said. "Anywhere."

The guy stressed the word "anywhere."

The guy seemed to be the one who was in charge of the little group. Besides the college-age girl, there were two boys about the same college age, all looking stunned. More than likely this had been some sort of field trip for a class and the older, long-haired guy was the professor.

The guy again stressed the word "anywhere," more than Benny wanted him to.

The other three nodded, all holding their cell phones as if they were lifelines. After walking a dozen blocks, Benny was starting to get the idea that no one was going to toss any of them a lifeline.

"Anyone try tuning in a radio?" Benny asked, something he

kicked himself for not doing at once back at the office. He clearly wasn't thinking as well as he seemed to think he was.

That wasn't a good sign and he needed to make sure he was extra careful.

The guy nodded. "Nothing. The internet is still working, so is Facebook and Twitter, but not one new post from anyone, anywhere in the world, that we can tell. We are searching. And no one, including any of our family across the country, is answering any of us."

Benny made himself take a deep breath and push back the panic from that thought. He figured this might have been city-wide, not worldwide.

That thought threatened to crack his cold, hard shell and he pushed it back down.

What the hell had happened?

He took another deep breath, then asked the same question again out loud.

"What the hell happened?"

"Are they all dead?" the young college-age girl asked, the look of panic in her blue eyes.

Benny had seen that look a number of times in soldiers' eyes in Iraq. She was about to flip and he wanted no part of that.

"They might be," Benny said. "I'd head off the island, get away from the city."

The professor-guy nodded.

"We can't drive and the subways aren't working," the girl said, her voice higher than a moment ago.

She was very close to going into complete panic.

The guy who seemed in charge of his little group said softly, "Let's walk."

He turned them toward the river. They stumbled in the direction he got them started in.

Then he looked back at Benny. "You coming?"

"Got to check on a few people first," Benny said.

He had no one to check on, but it was an easy lie to get out of going with them.

"We'll head south if you want to join us," the long-haired guy said.

"Thanks," Benny said to him. "I might."

Benny reached into his wallet and handed the guy his card. "Cell phone number. Call me if you hear anything or end up back this way if the phones are still working."

Benny had no intention at that moment of joining anyone, but better to leave the options open. At least this group seemed to be holding together, except for the girl.

The older guy nodded and tucked Benny's card into a pocket. "Good luck," the older guy said and followed his little flock.

Benny was starting to think it was the human race that needed the luck now. No one online, no emergency declared, and no announcements coming across any emergency bands or over the radio.

From anywhere on the planet.

Benny had a hunch that no help was coming. That group could walk all the way to Florida and never find help, other than other survivors.

Benny stood and looked around at all the death

surrounding him. He had a hunch the human race had just bought the farm in a really big way.

Clearly being down in the subway had saved a number of people, and him being in his vault had saved him from whatever killed all these people.

It hadn't been gas and it hadn't been an attack. That much was clear. He had read an article last month about some huge burst of energy that might take out the entire planet coming from some other sun. Maybe something like that had happened without warning.

Or maybe this had been an alien attack.

That thought made him smile. He had clearly watched far too many late-night movies. Maggie really liked those old bug-eyed monster movies. He had really liked when she sat on his couch watching television, giving him occasional glimpses of those wonderful white panties. It had been a fair trade.

He was fairly certain he was never going to know the answer to the question of what happened. And to be honest, he didn't much care. What he did care about was staying alive now that he had drawn the lucky straw.

He headed toward Broadway along 42nd Street, working his way among the bodies.

A number of dogs, still attached to their leashes were dead as well, but he caught a glimpse of a few cats still moving. So whatever had killed the humans had spared the cats. Strange.

Near some garbage cans he also saw a number of dead rats. Thankfully he wasn't going to have to deal with those.

He kept walking, just looking at everything, trying to get himself calmed down, if that was even slightly possible.

What was really creepy about the bodies was the lack of blood. All the bodies he had seen in the past had become bodies because of holes that let out a lot of blood. No one sprawled on the sidewalk had any more than a bump on the head or a slight bloody face from hitting their nose when they fell.

He wandered all the way over to Broadway, seeing only a few survivors picking their way through the streets of dead. He didn't talk with any of them, but instead turned and went up Broadway.

He had no idea why. He just needed to explore, see the city he loved totally dead, help the reality sink in completely.

Finally, a couple hours later, as the sun was starting to set, he found himself back at his loan company on Lexington.

It had been a nice little business, funded by investors to help those on the streets that needed help to get by with short-term, interest-free loans. He had felt good running the little shop, helping out people, and Madge had been fantastic at getting the business grants and donors to keep everything going.

He went into his little business and pulled both Madge and Maggie out onto the sidewalk and sat them with their backs against the front of the business, like they were looking out over the street on a cool summer's evening. He smoothed down Maggie's dress so her white panties didn't show.

He had been around enough dead bodies to know that in short order they would start smelling. No point in having Marge and Maggie smell up his office.

He stood on the sidewalk and looked in both directions,

suddenly realizing something that was very obvious. This entire city was going to be one stinking mess quicker than he wanted to think about. It was scheduled to not get hot for a week, which would help a little.

But not that much.

He had smelled his share of three-or-four-day-dead human bodies and didn't much care for it.

Yet in a city full of the dead, where could he go?

Where could he go in a world full of dead?

CHAPTER 4

After talking with the others for an hour or so, Gina had gone back to her apartment on the ship and the office in her apartment.

The apartment seemed, for the first time in a while, empty. She wished she had someone to talk with, to share all this with, but she didn't. In two hundred years, she had only had a dozen relationships, all fairly long-term, but none of them had really been right for her.

And none of them had been with other Seeders, so after a few years, since she didn't age, she had always moved on.

So now she lived alone and seldom dated. Being embedded in less-advanced cultures for a decade or two per mission sort of kept the possibility of relationships down. And she had gotten used to that fact.

Most of the time, she actually liked it that way.

Helping others was worth it to her. That was her passion

and what had made her sign up for this job. She sure didn't need the money anymore, since she hadn't spent hardly anything besides apartment costs in the last few hundred years.

But she didn't do this for the money. She did this as a calling, to help people improve themselves.

But on days like today, having someone close would have been nice.

She had the lights come up to just under bright and brought up some lively dance music as background to lighten her mood.

Her apartment was comfortable, with a small living room furnished in what she liked to call graduate school comfort. Huge overstuffed chairs, a long, deep couch, and a coffee table stacked high with reading material and files. One wall of the living room was a large screen, the other walls were covered in various cultures' art she had liked from her different missions.

She mostly used the living room for reading or watching movies she had collected from different planets. The apartment also had a nice kitchen where she cooked basic meals and a small bedroom. Another room off to one side of the living room functioned as her office.

The walls of her office were also decorated with pictures and art from various planets.

And some images of people, of children, families, she had helped along the way.

The apartment felt a lot like the one she had lived in while going to college on her home world to get her degrees in social science. But that apartment had been in a six-story building just down the hill from the university while this apartment was on a massive starship.

She had been on board the *Star Conscious* now for six months and the ship would remain in orbit being a support for all the embedded Seeders going into the planet below. She was glad of that, since that way she could come and go from this apartment when she wanted over the next ten years.

That would help her stay level, she knew, during the coming mission.

She now sat in her office, using a grid system over the island covered by the massive city below. That was her area, that island, and all the survivors on it.

That room she had been in as the ship first arrived in orbit would hold most of the survivors from that island city that the locals called Manhattan. But before the rest of the ships got here, she needed to track and make sure she knew where every person on the island was, so no one got missed.

She would put a tracker on each person in the *Star Conscious* computer for the extraction moment. The tracker was nothing more than a recording of each person's biometric signature and general location. The computer would do the rest in tracking them.

Right now, as the evening started to settle over the dead city on the surface and the automatic lights came on, most of the survivors had settled down. Only a few were still moving around, so it was easier for her to start tagging the survivors.

Her equipment in her office could allow her to zoom right in on each person, so close she could see facial expressions and often read their lips as to what they were saying.

She didn't think she would need to get in that close on any of the survivors. At least not this soon after the disaster. She just needed to start putting tracking on them, putting their biometric signatures into the computer so that they would not be missed.

She knew she was in for a long night.

The idea that she might miss someone just scared her to death.

An idea of what dreams she might have if she tried to sleep scared her even more.

CHAPTER 5

Benny went back inside his office as night started to take over and sat in his chair behind his desk. He put up his feet and tried to think while keeping the cold of the "emotion screen," as his counselor called it, in place. Breaking down now might just end up getting him as dead as everyone else.

Outside the car alarms had calmed down some and the city was actually much quieter than he ever remembered hearing it, even late at night.

He looked around at the business he had put his heart into since getting out of the service and sighed. "Not much to do here. I think you need to figure out what to do with the next part of your life, Benny. Right?"

No one answered. His voice just echoed and that seemed damn creepy as well.

He stood and headed back out into the light of the city.

Luckily, the electrical systems were still working, the stoplights still going through their cycles over piles of wrecked cars. The streetlights and building lights still made the night in the city seem like daylight. That was one of the many things he loved about this city. It never really got dark.

Now, more than likely, that wouldn't last very long without people maintaining the power systems and lines. First good heat wave of the summer and this place would be a smelling pile of dead meat without electricity.

He headed the five blocks to his apartment, walking carefully around the bodies.

His apartment, a place he liked in most times, felt unusually silent. He clicked on the television, hoping to find something or someone to tell him what happened.

Nothing.

Some stations that had automatic programming were running, but the rest were just dead air.

The radio was the same, so he finally tuned the radio to an automatic light jazz station and let it play just to have some background music to pretend that society still existed outside the walls.

Then, using his computer, another appliance that would soon be worthless, he pulled up some maps of the New York area and the area going south.

After an hour of studying those maps, he decided the idea was too stupid for words. Assuming he made the hike all the way to Florida, even taking some cars once he was outside of the city, what was he going to do down there with the alligators and snakes and rotting-in-the-sun bodies?

"Think, Benny, think!"

He couldn't think of one darned thing.

Nothing.

Then he figured he could go north, get away from all people in the woods, but he had never been one for camping. If he was going to rough it without power, he was going to do it in a plush apartment or suite. Bears shit in the woods, he liked indoor plumbing if he had a choice.

He then decided to make sure going south was as bad an idea as he had a hunch it was.

He started dialing friends he knew in Southern California from the service, another friend in Chicago from his college days, even an old girlfriend in Texas.

Again nothing.

He even dialed five of his old buddies who were still stationed overseas.

Not a one answered.

He dialed twenty people in total.

All machines or no answer.

Not rock-solid proof things were bad everywhere, but adding in the internet and television silence, enough for him.

He pushed the phone away and made himself take a deep breath, to make sure the panic would stay down.

Then he grabbed a yellow pad and asked, "What are you going to need to survive this summer and the following winter?"

Then he started making a list.

—He was going to need power for lights and air-conditioning and heat for long term.

—He was going to somehow need to figure out a way to get a place that he could hold back most of the smell until that passed, which was going to take some time and help from mother nature.

The bodies on the street would eventually dry out and mummify, which wouldn't smell as bad, but then when the rains came, the smell would return for a time.

—He was going to need a place to store food and lots of canned supplies.

—And considering the nut cases in this town that might still be alive, he was going to need a place he could protect.

—And from the faint glow out his window from the building on fire ten blocks up the street, he would need a place that wouldn't easily burn.

Maybe he could get a band of other survivors together who could work together to search for food and for defense.

He liked the sound of that.

He walked over to the window and stared toward the center of the city.

He stood there for a moment until suddenly he saw it.

The answer was right there in front of him. He knew exactly the place that fit the bill perfectly.

The Empire State Building.

Perfect.

He cooked himself a good steak dinner from his fridge and scanned the television and radio channels again as he ate, coming up blank yet again. Nothing was working besides automatic systems and those weren't going to last long at all.

Then he put on a light jacket with his trusty .45 in one pocket along with a flashlight and headed out.

At night, even with the lights of the city still completely on, the bodies looked even stranger piled and sprawled on the sidewalk.

He figured the Empire State Building had pretty much everything he would need. It was a secured building so he could defend it, it would have a pretty fine security system and extra supply of weapons for the guards, and it would have generators. In fact, he was betting it had lots of generators to run all those elevators in power failures.

He seemed to remember that the building had a lot of different elevators. Also it was high enough and windy enough that even at the worst of the smell, it should be survivable up high in the building with windows sealed.

The biggest problem was going to be clearing out the bodies that had died inside. He was going to need to do that quickly as soon as he made sure the building actually did have everything he needed.

It took him a good hour winding his way through the dead to reach the Empire State Building.

He stopped a block away and looked up at it. The damn building was a lot bigger than he remembered it.

Securing it was a crazy idea, but considering the situation, a crazy idea was exactly what he needed.

CHAPTER 6

G ina worked at her desk and monitor for almost five hours straight with only occasional breaks to get more coffee. She had three screens, one of which showed a map of the big island and the streets of the city, another had a simpler map with red dots showing each survivor.

And her main screen had an image full of green dots, showing which survivors she had tagged.

In those hours, she had managed to get the biometric signatures of every survivor she could find in the dead city, watching the number of red dots shrink as the green dots increased.

As the next day went by, the heat signatures of survivors would help her find even more, she knew.

She glanced at her screen and the green dots scattered

around the island, almost all not moving. There were three hundred and sixty survivors still on the island.

For the next ten days she would have to monitor the entire area carefully to make sure to include anyone who came and went.

All over the ship she knew that others were also having long nights, working to track every survivor in their areas.

Four other large starships were now in orbit with the *Star Conscious*, three of them Seeder ships. All five ships were working on the same task she was doing over various parts of the world. There were billions dead, but by best estimates, over two million survivors.

Their mission was to not miss a person for this rescue from the second deadly electromagnetic pulse. If they rescued everyone, it would give the population of this planet a huge jump forward in a restart.

She spent another fifteen minutes going over everything, making sure she hadn't missed anyone for the night.

She hadn't.

Now she had to get some rest somehow. She would come back to this in a few hours as the sun came up over the city below and start tracking closely all of the people below to see their situations.

She dumped out the last of her cold coffee, slipped into her exercise clothes, and jumped to the ship's gym. It was a huge room with a hundred different machines, a very long running track, a climbing wall, and courts for various racket games. She liked the weight machines and did a quick fifteen-minute workout alone. She almost never had the big exercise area to herself. It felt good.

And eerily silent.

When she finished, she felt better, her muscles from so much time at the machine now loose. She jumped back to her apartment and took a quick shower to try to wash away some of the day, then got into her running shorts, a light exercise shirt, and her slippers.

That was her normal evening-at-home clothes and even though this was far from a normal evening, she wanted to pretend it was.

She went with a snack plate of crackers and cheese to the big comfortable couch in her living room.

There she clicked on a comedy movie done on the last planet she had been embedded in. She had seen it before and knew it was good. Right now she needed something to clear the images of that dead city and all those bodies from her mind.

If that was ever going to be possible.

She stretched out on her couch, a soft cloth pillow under her head, a thin blanket over her legs and feet. She started up the movie and took a few crackers, munching slowly, focusing on the movie she had already seen.

Somewhere in the first third of the movie she dozed off. Thankfully, the movie playing kept most of the nightmares back.

Not all of them, but most.

CHAPTER 7

By eleven in the evening, Benny had borrowed the keys off a guard's body and found the security room. It had twenty monitors that all seemed to be working.

Twenty different views of the area around the building and the lobbies. And a couple of the monitors cycled through eight images as he watched.

Nothing was moving on any of the monitors.

Nothing.

For a short time he just kept staring at them, looking from one to another, expecting something to move.

Finally he shook his head.

"Benny, you've got yourself into a real mess this time."

His voice echoed in the bedroom-sized security room.

Staring at all the bodies showing on those cameras, he almost decided to just pack and head for Florida. Or maybe he could go north into the Canadian wilderness, join the bears shitting in the woods.

Then he shook that thought away.

This city was his home and he would be damned if he was going to let the fact that most everyone was dead scare him off.

It took him another half hour in the security room to clear out the three guard's bodies filling the chairs and a fourth guard in a back break room. Then he spent an hour finding all the generators for all the floors and the ones that ran the elevators. The generators had more than enough fuel, and when that ran out, he could re-supply easily from all the cars and trucks on the street.

From a diagram in the guardroom, he could tell there was a good-sized water tank up high that had electrical pumps. He was going to have to check every room to make sure all the water was turned off so that didn't drain out when the power shut off.

The Empire State Building was all offices and meeting rooms and tourist stuff. No apartments, so he would have to find a really high office and clean that out and set up an apartment. That would be easy to do.

He hoped.

He had a hunch none of what he was thinking of doing was going to be easy.

For the next hour, he went around taking all the keys and guns from the dead guards and then locking the five main entrances to the building. That felt weird, like he was locking out the dead, but if he wanted to be secure, no point in taking any chances that some other survivors had this idea.

The last thing he needed were survivors with more guns than he had. And in New York, nut cases with guns scared him more than almost anything else.

Outside the doors, the lights of the city looked very strange on all the people scattered dead on the sidewalks.

He went back to the main security area and spent the rest of the night making sure he knew all the details of the building, or at least as much as he could find.

He didn't want to be on an elevator with no chance of rescue when the power went out. He needed to know that the back-up generators would kick in and if that didn't happen, how to do an emergency escape from the elevator. He had a hunch he was going to be spending a lot of time in those elevators. Being trapped alive in one with no chance of rescue scared him cold.

Somewhere along the way, he fell asleep for a few hours on a cot in a side room off the security area.

He didn't even remember lying down.

CHAPTER 8

Gina awoke sweating on the couch, the light blanket twisted around her feet. Her mouth was dry and her short hair was plastered to her head.

She pushed away any thought of trying to remember any dream and managed to get untangled and get to her feet. The screen was blank, so the movie had ended and the system had shut down.

She clicked it off and glanced at a clock near the screen. She had been asleep for three hours. The sun would be coming up on the city below. She needed to get back to work.

She headed for the bathroom for another shower, then to her kitchen to get a few bagels with cream cheese and a large glass of orange juice. That was her breakfast of choice most mornings and it got her going.

Usually she headed to the ship's gym after breakfast to do

her regular hour-long exercise routine, but today she would skip that.

Too much to do, too many lives at stake.

She got back into her office to her screens and discovered that while she had slept, five of her tagged survivors had left the island. She transferred them to the person monitoring the area they were in.

There were also six new red dots on her screen and she quickly tagged them. She had no idea where they had come from. More than likely deep underground, although her system could penetrate through a hundred feet of rock and any building.

But there was a good chance they had been farther underground than that last night.

She sat eating her breakfast while methodically checking her survivors to make sure they were tagged correctly.

She had just finished her breakfast and downed the last of her orange juice when one of her green lights winked out.

She instantly focused her tracking on it, afraid of what she might find, but knowing she had to look anyway.

The survivor had been a man about fifty. He had taken a gun to his head while sitting next to his wife and two teenage kids who had died while eating.

She felt sick, looking at the scene of death like a snooping angel.

She made a note with shaking hands that he was dead and then pulled back so she didn't have to look at the scene any more.

She knew, and everyone who was doing her job had been

briefed, that over the next ten days, while they were tracking the survivors for the rescue and waiting for all the ships to arrive, many survivors would either be killed or take their own lives.

She just hadn't expected it to happen so soon.

She pushed back from her desk and took her orange juice glass and plate she had used for the bagels to the kitchen.

Then she just stood there, her head down over the sink, shaking.

She had been alive for almost two hundred years, had seen many things in the cultures she had worked, but she had no doubt the next nine days until rescue were going to be some of the longest and hardest days she had ever lived.

And then after that, it would only get worse.

After that, she would be down there, on those streets, with the survivors, trying to help.

CHAPTER 9

An alarm woke Benny up.

He scrambled to the screens in the main security room, at first not remembering where he was or what had happened.

Then he saw all the bodies and nothing moving. The sun was slowly bringing light to the city.

The first full day of death was dawning.

An alarm was flashing and ringing like an insane doorbell that it was time to open the doors.

He shut it off, dropping the room back into welcome silence.

He went back to the cot where he had passed out a few hours before and clicked on a radio there. It gave him no more hope than it had yesterday.

Outside, it looked overcast and cool. That was good for the

moment, since it would slow down the body decay slightly on the people in the streets.

And keep most of them from heating up in the sun, swelling, and exploding from the expanding gas inside of them. He had seen that a few times in Iraq as well.

He hoped to never see it again.

He banged open a candy machine in the break room and breakfast consisted of a couple packs of nuts and a Diet Coke.

From what he could tell from the monitors, there had to have been at least three or four hundred people in this building when humanities number came up. No way he was going to move all of them ahead of when they would start smelling.

He was just going to have to go up high, to the 102 Floor Observatory, and work his way down, clearing every body he could find from as many top floors as he could.

About a third of the way up, a person had to change elevators and there were a lot of bodies in that lobby area, so he just figured more there wouldn't hurt.

But when he got to that lobby, he decided that was a bad idea. He was going to have to go through that transition floor all the time. He needed to clear that first.

He went down three floors from the transition area and into a huge office suite. There were a good twenty bodies in the big room that he could see.

Using a large fire ax, he broke out some of the windows in an office there, letting in the morning-chilled wind from outside. The office had a door on it that he could close after he was finished.

Then, one-by-one, he dragged all the bodies in that large

office area to the window and just dumped them out, leveraging them up over the edge and turning away as they fell.

After about thirty bodies, a couple of which could have used less pasta when alive, he decided he was going to need a better system. He wouldn't have a back after a short time.

Plus touching the dead bodies that much gave him the creeps.

He went down to the building mail and shipping room and got a large cart used to haul heavy boxes. Then on the service elevator, he went all the way to the top.

It took him two hours to clear the two-dozen people on the top observation deck and take them down a dozen floors to another empty office suite, where he again broke out a window in an office that could be shut tight after he was done. This time he just stacked the poor souls near the window to take care of later.

He felt bad that he wasn't treating the dead in a more respectful fashion, but at this point, his own survival was far, far more important. And that depended on getting the dead out of the building as soon as he could.

By eleven in the morning, he knew that stacking those bodies there wouldn't help his situation at all. He had to toss them outside. Which meant that by the time he got done clearing out the bodies in this building, there would be a stack of human flesh a story tall around the north base.

He would be living on a pile of the dead.

But again he could think of no other choice.

But he could toss them out only on the north side, leaving the other three sides open.

Like they used to say in the service, he was already walking dead. Not a way to keep from making a mistake and getting himself injured or killed. He was going to need more food and more rest, if that was possible before he went on.

He went back down to the security area and did a check of the area outside the building.

Just death.

No movement.

He ate a quick lunch of some guard's sandwich stored in the fridge and then took another nap. Two hours later, he was just about ready to go again when his cell phone in his pocket rang and scared hell out of him.

"Yeah," he said after he scrambled to get it to his ear.

"This is the man you met yesterday with the three college kids," the voice on the other end said.

"Find anything?" Benny asked, for a moment excited at the idea that he might have been wrong about everyone being dead.

"Nothing," the man said. "We're coming back to the city. It's where we all live, doesn't seem right leaving it. You got any ideas on where to hole up to get through the summer and all the smell?"

Benny's stomach twisted in disappointment, then he pushed that aside as he had been pushing all feeling aside since this started.

He glanced at the security cameras showing room after room of bodies and shrugged. Why not? He could use the help.

"I'm setting up the Empire State Building," Benny said. "It

won't burn, it's got generators, a great security system, and a good water supply. It can be defended."

"And it's high enough to escape some of the smell," the guy said.

Benny was impressed. He had been worrying about the same thing.

"You and your merry band want to join me?" Benny asked. "There's a lot of work to do."

"It will take us about three hours to get there," the professor said. "Thanks."

"Pick up anyone else you see that looks sane along the way," Benny said. "This is one big building. And go to the South Entrance. I'll be waiting there in three hours."

"Okay," the professor said.

"And one more thing. Stay away from the building on the north side."

"Why?" he asked, then before Benny could tell him, the professor said, "Oh, I understand."

This guy really was smart. That was good. It was going to take Benny's street smarts and military training and the professor's brains to get any of them alive through the coming year.

"Three hours, call me if you get stuck or run into problems."

"Three hours," he said and hung up.

Benny once again checked the television and radio. Nothing.

At least he was going to have help.

CHAPTER 10

A s the day wore on, Gina was handed four survivors coming back onto the island from the south, and in turn she had handed off more than a dozen leaving the city, most headed north.

From her original three hundred and sixty, she was down to three hundred and twenty-two.

From the maps of the area, going north made sense, since in that direction was more wilderness and fewer people. It would be a lot easier in the wilderness to survive the smell of all the death that was coming.

One-by-one, she checked in on the survivors in her area. Most of them had gone home. Many were just sitting in shock next to a dead loved one.

A few were working to fortify and remove dead bodies from upper areas of apartment buildings and one man was working to remove bodies from one of the tallest buildings in the city.

There were only a few people working with another person. Almost everyone worked alone and she couldn't imagine that. It showed the really true survival ability of the human race.

The man in the big building seemed to have been moving almost constantly since she awoke and her interest kept going to him. She didn't focus in close because he was always moving dead bodies and tossing them out windows. She didn't need to see that up close, but she admired what he was doing in trying to survive.

And his strength.

She forced herself to take both a lunch break away from her screens and a dinner break. She needed to just sit in her kitchen and focus on eating and not thinking about what was happening on the planet below.

Both meals had been nothing special, just a sandwich and a drink and a piece of fruit, but it was enough.

After her dinner break, she headed to the gym again for a short workout, then, after a quick shower, she took a cup of tea back with her to the office and to watch as many survivors worked to get ready for another night.

And many, many more survivors just sat, doing nothing.

She honestly wasn't sure what she would be doing if this had happened to her home world and she had survived.

She hoped she would be one working to survive.

But she wasn't sure.

CHAPTER 11

enny took some lumber from the maintenance area and went back up to the floor where he had broken out the window in the office. There he spent an hour building a ramp for the shipping cart that slanted slowly up to the broken window.

Then he went back to the floor under the top observation platform and worked his way down, room-by-room, office-by-office, floor-by-floor, using the cart to take the bodies he found to the ramp and dumping them out the window. Luckily for him, some of those floors were empty, thanks to the high rents for the place.

Or a slow day at the office.

In one office, it made him sad when he found twenty very attractive women, slumped to the floor or over their desks. He would have dated any of them. And that thought made him miss Maggie and her white panties.

He even missed Madge.

He just hoped that some women survived besides that panicked college girl. With luck, he and other survivors would build a nice little community right here in the Empire State building.

With luck.

He found a nice hide-a-bed couch in one executive's office on the eighty-ninth floor and decided that was where he would bunk for the night later. It had a really nice bathroom and shower and he was really needing a shower after all those bodies and work.

He had had no idea how much work it was going to be to move around dead human weight. People who had done that for a living before were amazing.

Exhausted, he went downstairs to the south entrance at three hours, making sure to take the .45 tucked in his pocket.

No sign of the professor and his class, so he went across the street to a deli and got some great roast beef from the fridge and made himself a sandwich. He was really going to miss fresh meat.

He got enough food for three solid meals tomorrow and went back across the street and put the food in the fridge in the security room.

The deli had three bodies in it and another near the door, but he just didn't have the energy to do anything with the bodies at the moment. But he would have to, since that deli had a full back room of supplies and some nice freezers full of meat. He figured he could get a couple of those freezers across the street and hooked up to a generator and maybe have meat for the winter.

He was back inside the lobby of the Empire State Building and was about to lock the door when he saw the professor and his three charges winding their way along the sidewalk.

They all looked tired and clearly depressed, and the girl had lost her backpack along the way.

He propped the door open and waited for them, chewing on the roast beef sandwich with horseradish, which he had to admit, tasted wonderful.

"Thanks, Benny," the professor said, extending his hand. "My name is Professor C.M. Green." He laughed, sadly. "Not sure what I'm a professor of anymore."

He had managed to pull back his long hair and tie it, and Benny could tell the professor had been a gym rat. He was strong, of that Benny had no doubt. The professor had a firm grip, but Benny could tell that the last day had really worn on him.

Benny was fairly certain he looked just as bad.

The professor quickly introduced the two college boys. The redhead with bright freckles who stood about six foot was called David. The other kid, shorter with a lot of pimples was Freddy. Both looked like they could use some muscle and about fifty pounds. The girl was named Candice. She had long blonde hair, long fingernails, and the remains of some makeup on her blue eyes. She looked like she was about to pass out.

"You had any real food?" Benny asked them.

The professor shook his head. "Just snacks is all."

"So that's job one," Benny said.

He had them leave their stuff just inside the building entrance, tossed the professor a group of keys from a guard, locked up the building, then headed across the street to the deli.

"Boys," Benny said, "can you clear out those bodies, move them a little ways down the sidewalk, maybe about thirty steps, while the professor and I fix you something to eat."

Both boys looked horrified that they would have to touch a dead body and the professor didn't look too pleased himself.

"Do it this way," Benny said, grabbing the man's body near the door by both feet right at the ankle. Then Benny just dragged the body away from the door and down the sidewalk. The body's clothes bunched up some as Benny went, but not enough to slow him down.

"Don't try to pick them up," Benny said, still tugging on the body down the walk, "and if you don't want to use your bare hands, there's a store two doors down that has leather gloves. Bring me and the professor back two pair of larges each as well."

Benny stopped dragging the body, then led the professor and the girl into the deli as the two boys went for gloves.

"There's a lot of work to get that building ready," Benny said as they went in behind the counter.

"I can't even imagine," he said.

"You won't have to imagine," Benny said. "You're going to get to see it for yourself as soon as we're done eating."

The boys cleared out the bodies, each grabbing one leg and moving quickly. Then they all sat and ate sandwiches with cold pop.

The professor described how far they had walked before turning back. They had stayed the night in a furniture store, but most of them hadn't slept much.

All of them had families they were convinced were dead, and the professor had a wife. "We're all going to need to find our families and check on them," he said. "It's why we came back."

Benny nodded. His only family had been Madge and Maggie. Both his parents had died in a boating accident while he was in Iraq. He knew Maggie and Madge were dead. He would have looked for them as well if he hadn't known. Especially Maggie.

"I can understand that," Benny said.

The professor nodded thanks.

"Any idea at all what caused this?" Benny asked as the conversation lagged.

"Quasar pulse," Freddy said.

"Aliens," David said.

The professor shook his head. "All kinds of theories, no facts."

Benny nodded. "Well back to the task of survival then. We need to get as much of the building cleared and set up before things turn really sour."

"You mean everything smells?" Candice asked.

"Worse than you can imagine," Benny said. "We'll work some more tonight, and then we all need some rest."

He turned to the professor. "How about tomorrow you take a student and go out one at a time to find that person's family?

And maybe look for more sane people to join us. The rest of us will keep working."

"That's a really good plan," the professor said, trying and failing to sound upbeat. "Everyone up for that?"

They all just nodded and kept eating.

If nothing else, this was the most well-behaved and smallest class Benny had ever seen.

CHAPTER 12

G ina watched after dinner as the four that had come back into the city joined the man working alone in the big building. Somehow they had known he was there. Maybe related or something and able to get in touch.

So far, all the systems in the city seemed to be staying up. But as the night fell over the city for the second time since all the death, Gina knew that it wouldn't be long before those lights would never come on again.

But pulling back, the view from above of the island city was stunning at night, the city looking alive and vibrant, at least from orbit.

As the sun started to fall, she had green lights wink and go dark on her board.

She checked each one because she had to. It was her job.

Six total. Three had gone to a roof of a building and just walked off the edge.

She knew this was happening all over the planet right now. She just wished they could get the survivors off faster, give them some hope, if not just for a moment.

But right now there were less than twenty ships in orbit over all the death. She knew there would need to be almost a thousand ships to get all the survivors, and many of those rescue ships wouldn't arrive until the last minute. Many were coming from another sector of this galaxy at full speed.

After another two hours, all the survivors in her area seemed to have settled down, including the five now together in the big building. So she went and took another shower to try to clear away the day, then went to her couch again and started up the same comedy movie she had on the night before.

She didn't need to be entertained. She just needed noise and some life.

She fell asleep in twenty minutes.

And the only dream she had that she could remember was of watching a person's face with a green light on the person's forehead. Then the light winked out and the person slumped to the ground.

And she had to turn away and do nothing, because there was nothing she could do.

CHAPTER 13

A fter finishing the sandwiches and closing up the deli, Benny took the professor and his charges up to the security room and made sure they all knew the same things he did about the emergency generators and how to escape if stuck in an elevator when the power went out.

Then pulling the professor aside, Benny suggested that the two boys start working on clearing out the main lobbies downstairs, dragging the bodies away from the main doors and down the sidewalk a distance, that sort of thing. And that the professor and Candice start on the floor Benny had left off hauling bodies out, check every bathroom and lunchroom in every office to make sure the water was turned off. Even the public bathrooms in the lobbies and if there were any sinks or bathrooms in any basement areas.

"What are you going to do?" the professor asked after he

sent the two boys off with their assignments and instructions to call him on his cell if they needed him.

"I am going to keep working my way down clearing bodies."

The professor just nodded.

Benny decided that first the three of them needed to go all the way back to the top, then start down from there, double-checking to make sure he hadn't missed any body in a maintenance area, or in a back office or rest room, and that all the water was turned off on those upper floors.

Benny showed the professor and Candice his cart set-up and ramp in the office with the broken window when they reached that floor.

Neither said a word.

Then the two of them went off checking the water and Benny kept working his way down, one body, one floor at a time. By the time two hours had gone by and the lights of the city were on full, Benny had the top thirty floors completely cleared of bodies.

And he was exhausted. He knew they all were.

He had scouted the neighborhood a little, mostly with the exterior security cameras, and he knew there was another restaurant nearby, so all five of them headed there to scrounge for food.

A couple stores down from the restaurant, they found bedding, and in a neighboring store they all found a change of clothes.

They cleared the bodies out of both places in only minutes,

since Benny figured they were going to need to use both places in the future.

Benny was starting to feel better by the minute.

It had only been a little over a day since the world ended and he had a hunch this new way of living just might work. They all might actually have a way to survive, with enough help.

And a little more time with the weather staying cool and the power staying on.

Benny doubted that would happen, but he figured a guy could hope.

CHAPTER 14

Over the next few days, Gina fell into a routine. She would crawl off the couch and check on the survivors in her city, finding any that had died in the night, and seeing if she had anyone new, or if others had left the city.

After the third day, all the others who were doing her job for other areas under the *Star Conscious* had a meeting. There were forty of them and they all looked as tired and worn out as she was feeling.

The upshot of the meeting was that after three days, every survivor on the planet had been identified by all the ships in orbit and tagged. As soon as the other ships got here, the survivors would be taken off the planet and out of danger for the time of the second electromagnetic pulse.

They were told to start getting to know the survivors who

looked like they would make it, the ones they could help, to figure out the best way to help the survivors after the rescue.

She wasn't willing to do that just yet. Too many were still dying.

By the fourth day, she had under three hundred survivors alive on the island. And she knew that a few more of them didn't have much longer to live, since they hadn't been eating or moving in days.

The five survivors in the big building she still watched from a distance, and four others in another tall building were working on it to clear bodies and make it livable. More than likely that would be the two groups she would work to help.

All the other survivors huddled inside apartments or underground in the subway system, some setting up camps in the stalled trains.

Except for checking on those that died, she kept her focus above the city, thinking of each person at the moment as a green light. That helped her nightmares some.

And she didn't have to see the bodies that littered everything slowly starting to decompose.

She was going to embed in that city to help the survivors, and right now, she refused to think about what that smell was going to be like.

Since all Seeders could teleport, she would be able to return to her apartment here at any point, but she had no doubt that would not be enough by any stretch.

She knew those survivors below would need her help after the rescue. She knew that deep down. But she had no idea why she had applied to do this.

CHAPTER 15

Benny was stunned that Mother Nature and the electric company conspired to help them some. It remained fairly cool, the nights almost chilly, and the power stayed on.

For five days, he and the Professor and his charges prepared the big building as much as they could.

After a few hundred bodies dumped through windows, Benny was just numb to what he was doing.

And after the first few days, they were all wearing masks and tossing their clothes out after working. Every night Benny took a long, hot shower to try to clear the smell from his nose.

They finally got every body they could find out of the big building by day four. Benny was stunned it had been done. It was a very large building.

The city was starting to smell in general, so after clearing the bodies from the entire building, Benny turned their focus to stocking up on bedding, food, clothing, and just about anything else they thought they might need and could get on carts or carry.

Pretty soon they would just lock the doors and move up into the top floors. And after the power went out, they would run the generators for those floors, keeping them at a comfortable temperature through the summer.

Benny took the top office floor as his apartment, and the professor and his three kids stocked up the floor five down from his, since there were six bathrooms and lots of offices that could be made into bedrooms there.

From what Benny understood, they had spread out and each had a large area and a private bathroom.

Benny wanted them to be prepared for fifty or more people living in the building instead of just five, even though they hadn't seen anyone else in days. And the professor agreed.

So even after they had more than enough, they stocked food and blankets and propane heaters and lighting and everything else on a dozen different floors.

One day, David asked Benny why they were doing that.

"The moment the lights go out," Benny said, "and we keep some lights on in this building up high, people from all over will see us. We need to be ready for people to join us."

David had only nodded to that.

All the kids and the professor had found their families, all dead.

And every-so-often Benny would run across one of the kids crying. Nothing he could say to cheer them up. They were either going to make it or they weren't.

He had become very cold through all this, much more than he had ever been before.

His counselor had taught him that. He had decided after that session with the counselor that Benny would be one of the soldiers that made it.

And he would make it this time as well.

The young girl, Candice, just slowly withdrew, working and eating less and less, no matter what any of them said or tried to do to cheer her up.

Benny had seen that before in soldiers on the battlefield. He had no idea what to do about it.

On the fifth morning she vanished, going out the south door before any of them got up.

Benny had no doubt she wouldn't be back, but the professor wanted to go in search of her.

Benny stopped him at first with one simple statement speech. "It's safe out there. She knows where we are. If she wants to come back, she will. Give her until tomorrow before we go looking for her."

Benny doubted she would return, but he might be wrong. He hoped he would be.

The professor agreed and gave her the time and didn't go out looking for her. But the next day he and the boys went out into the smell. The professor said they had to do something.

Benny knew that feeling as well.

But it was one damn big city out there full of dead people, so he held out no hope.

CHAPTER 16

Gina just happened to be at her screens, watching the survivors green dots when one of the five from the big building in the center of town left. The other four didn't seem to be moving.

She focused her scan down on the moving survivor, surprised to find she was watching a young college-age girl wearing a mask against the smell, winding her way through the dead bodies on the street.

The young girl seemed to be staggering more than walking and Gina didn't like the looks of that at all.

Gina focused in on the girl's face as much as she could and could see the look of shock and despair in the girl's eyes. This girl was going off to die, Gina had no doubt.

And there was still a good five days until the rescue.

Gina followed the girl for the next hour as she worked

through the bodies, finally entering a large building with no survivors in it.

The girl went up the elevator to the eleventh floor and into an apartment there.

Gina could see there were two bodies in the apartment, both still in fairly decent shape because the air-conditioning in the apartment must have still been working.

Gina watched as the young girl sat down on the couch facing where one man sprawled on the floor and a woman lay sprawled in the kitchen.

The girl sat there for a few minutes, then went down the hall to a bedroom and crawled into a bed that must have clearly been hers before the disaster.

She pulled the blankets up to her chin and closed her eyes.

Gina knew exactly what had happened.

The young girl had gone home to be with her dead parents.

Gina switched back to the four others in the big building and for the first time focused down on them.

Two were young boys about the girl's age, another was a man with long hair, and the fourth man just flat took her breath away.

It was if an electrical shock had come through the screen and pushed her back in her chair.

He was clearly the one in charge. He had short dark hair and had shaved, something many of the survivors had not done. He wore jeans and a muscle shirt that clearly showed off how strong he was.

She glanced back at her records. He was the one that had first started cleaning out the building on his own.

She just stared at him, stunned that she was having such a reaction. Normally a man never really caught her attention. Over the last few centuries, there had been a few that had twisted her heart, and a dozen or more short relationships, but never had she felt a reaction like this to just seeing a man.

After a short discussion as Gina watched, they all nodded and seemed to go back to work.

Gina figured that they knew where the girl had gone and were going to give her time. That was the right decision for someone in shock and mourning as that young girl clearly was.

Gina followed them, becoming more impressed by the minute that all four of them were fine, now working to build a future in the big building.

As she followed them, they went out into the city streets and worked to get more bedding, more food, more supplies from nearby stores.

All four of them had carts and they worked to stock floors where they did not live.

Clearly one of them, more than likely the man she could barely keep her eyes off of, was setting up the big building to hold a lot more than five.

Wow, he was good-looking.

And clearly smart.

She spent the next hour just watching him like she was beside him.

And for the first time, she actually wanted to be down there, in all that death, talking with him, getting to know him.

How was that even possible?

CHAPTER 17

The power cut out on the tenth day and, as Benny had expected, the heat started to climb to oppressive levels, making going outside into all the death just about impossible.

All the bodies along the sidewalks were bloated inside their cloths and impossible to look at. Benny again just thanked the luck that the rats and other rodents had all been killed. Otherwise, there would have been no staying in the city with the rats having unlimited food supply.

Benny had them all go to using propane lanterns and climbing stairs. He didn't want to take any chances at this point on elevators run by a generator until they tested everything. They could do that tomorrow.

Benny had set up a portable generator on a balcony outside of the office suite that he had converted to a very large apartment, with a big screen television and a movie library that would take him ten years to watch if he never stopped.

He had all the staircases boarded and sealed on his floor except for one, and that one he had steel bars locking it at night. And he had no doubt he had enough firepower to hold off a pretty good-sized attack.

Not that he thought one was coming. He actually doubted it was, but in the Gulf he had seen his share of the underside of humanity. And New York clearly had its share as well. He had survived this, which meant scum might have as well. Not everyone was going to be nice guys like the professor and his kids.

When the power went out, Benny made sure all outside and front doors were locked again, then set up alarms in the security room that would ring on his floor and the professor's floor if anyone banged on the outside door.

He also set up the exterior and lobby camera systems with motion sensors to run on generators. If anything at all moved near a door, the alarm would sound and they would see who it was.

Four days before, while it was still fairly cool out, the professor and the boys had gone out looking for Candice. They had come back depressed and smelling so bad, Benny just let them go take showers without a word.

The next day, because the two boys were still depressed, Benny and the professor went out again, without luck.

Candice had vanished.

Benny felt bad, but it didn't surprise him. Some people were survivors, others were not.

On the day after the power went out, over a light lunch, they got talking about what had happened again and what was going to happen.

"The aliens will come to rescue us," David said.

Benny shook his head and asked David, "Why would you say that?"

David shrugged. "They've been taking our kind to another planet for centuries. They knew we would be destroyed. They planned for it and will come back to help us."

"And you know all this how?" Benny asked as the professor just smiled, clearly having heard all this before.

"He doesn't," Freddy said. "If the aliens caused all this, they just missed a few of us and will be back to finish the job so they will have the planet to themselves."

"No, they will rescue us," David said.

"Kill us," Freddy said.

The professor said nothing.

Benny quickly changed the subject.

CHAPTER 18

For the last four days before the rescue, Gina no longer dreamed of death, but of the man with the black hair, dark eyes, and strong arms.

He seemed almost scary smart in how he went about preparing the big building. She was so looking forward to meeting him, but she wasn't sure what she was going to say. And that made her feel like a young kid again back in school.

She hadn't felt that way in two hundred years.

Besides what could she say after he had lived through those ten days? "Hi, I'm an alien and I'm here to rescue you for only a few hours before putting you back?"

She would have to think of something much better than that.

A lot better.

And then after she went to the surface to help them, she would have to think of yet another way to meet him.

But meet him twice she would. She was going to make sure of that.

Three days after the young girl left the group in the big building, it was clear she was never going back. The long-haired man and the two younger boys went out looking for her wearing gas masks to help hold back the smell.

Gina watched them carefully every step.

The first place they had gone was to where the young girl was hiding. They clearly had known her home address.

When the young girl had heard them coming, she had hid under her bed, curled inside a blanket. She did not want to be found.

Gina yelled at her screens, trying to shout through space that all they had to do was look under the bed. The girl was there and she needed help.

The long-haired man and the two boys didn't see her and left.

For an instant Gina considering jumping to the girl's apartment and making a lot of noise so the long-haired man and the two boys would return, but all the people in her job had strict orders to not go to the surface until after the rescue.

So she just watched.

When they left, the young girl got back out from under the bed and crawled back into bed, pulling the blankets over her head.

She had been eating some, so she would survive until rescue, but not much longer. Gina would try to do something to help her after rescue.

Gina looked at the tally of the green lights in her area. Just over two hundred and eighty survivors left.

But over half of those were alone just as the young girl was. They would make it to rescue, but not much longer after that when they were returned.

After the rescue, when Gina embedded on the surface, she might be able to find and help more of them besides the blonde girl. But she wondered if they even wanted help.

She would have to figure out which ones did want help during the rescue. And work with those. Maybe get them to the big building run by the most handsome man she had ever seen.

On the day before the rescue, she went to the big banquet-like room where all the survivors from her area would be transported. It would hold them, without a problem.

She double-checked on setting up showers that had special chemicals in the water to kill the smell. She made sure that all of them would have fresh clothing if they wanted it. And she worked with the medical staff to make sure there would be enough help there for the injured and those who needed to be sedated.

The extremely injured and near dead would not be sent back to the surface, but instead would be taken as refugees to another nearby planet. But everyone else would be sent back.

One wall of the big room was clear and looked out at the beautiful planet below. That view would help some of the survivors realize where they were.

Others, she knew, that view would shock. Again, medical would be ready.

Almost all of the survivors in her area would be asleep

when they were taken, since the time would be right before sunrise. That would help some as well, she hoped.

The entire rescue was going to only take about ten hours.

Ten very long hours for some survivors, ten very short hours for others. But none of them would remember it.

She went back to her apartment and got ready for the rescue, making careful notes of the locations of everyone and what they looked like so she could talk with them when they arrived.

If she was going to help these people, she had a lot of work to do both before and after they arrived in that big room.

THE RESCUE

THE RESCUE

CHAPTER 19

One moment Benny had been sound asleep on the big bed he had managed to get into the top floor office complex, the next he found himself standing beside the professor and the two boys with hundreds of other very tired and scared-looking humans who had survived the destruction of the world.

Some were wearing full clothes, others were wearing very little. Clearly all of them had been as asleep as he had been.

Luckily, he had been sleeping in sweat pants and a body shirt just in case. The light carpet under his bare feet was warm and slightly soft.

The room, at first glance, seemed like a normal hotel banquet room.

He looked quickly around him, but saw no real danger, just a bunch of very confused, sick, and smelly people.

"What the hell?" Benny asked, more to himself than anyone.

"We're in orbit above our city," David said, pointing at the big wall.

Benny turned and damn near dropped to the floor as his knees got wobbly.

They were in orbit.

Holy shit!

How had he got here?

Or someone had done a pretty good fake show of being in orbit on a huge wall. He wanted to try to believe that, but he knew he couldn't.

He was in orbit.

He could see that sunrise was working its way across the Atlantic toward the East Coast and there were very few clouds in the sky, meaning it was going to be a hot summer's day below if what he was seeing was real.

A very large if.

His mind would not accept it.

Could not accept it.

"That's amazing," Freddy said, his voice almost a whisper.

"I was right," David said. "The aliens are here to rescue us."

"Perfect," Benny said, staring out that window as more people around them noticed the view as well. "Are we in the frying pan or in the fire?"

"I'm guessing fire," the professor said.

"We're lunch," Freddy said.

"I doubt they have a cookbook," David said.

Benny had no idea what they were talking about, but it

didn't sound good that they suddenly found themselves in orbit in a ship and the two kids who liked science fiction were talking about aliens eating humans.

The noise and the smell stunned him as the people in the room started to shout and panic a little.

Numbers of people just fainted or dropped to the carpeted floor and sat there, their hands covering their faces.

Benny made himself take a deep breath and actually look around.

Except for the giant wall looking out into space, this room could have been any banquet room in any hotel. High ceilings with off-white paint, overhead lights, carpet on the floor.

Benny pushed back the feeling of panic trying to creep up his throat. He wasn't sure what there was to panic about, since most of the planet below had already been wiped out.

He honestly wasn't sure what could be worse, but he had a hunch he was about to find out.

Then one of the doors on one side of the room slid back and a dozen more people strode into the room.

They were far from alien.

In fact, one woman looked directly at him and then nodded and smiled as if she knew him.

He managed to catch his breath.

He was on an alien ship, after the world had ended, and he was having a reaction to some woman who walked into the room.

A real reaction.

A lust reaction.

All of the new arrivals looked as human as he was, only they were all clearly more rested and clean.

The woman wore a white blouse with the sleeves rolled up, jeans, and tennis shoes. She had really short, black hair and skin that contrasted with the black hair. She didn't seem to be any older than he was.

And she clearly worked out.

Around Benny the room quieted and calmed some as everyone turned to watch the new arrivals.

The woman with the short black hair stood to one side of the stage, clearly concerned as she looked around at everyone. One man jumped up on a low stage. You could have heard the old pin drop in that room, even on the carpeted floor.

The guy looked totally human. He had on a dress shirt, business slacks, and dress shoes. He could have been one of the Wall Street clones on a day off for all Benny could tell.

"Fine people of the great city of New York," he said in perfect English. "Very sorry to startle you like this from your sleep. What caused the disaster you have been living through was a pulsar blast of intense electromagnetic radiation. The next, and final wave off the pulsar will be hitting Earth in just under four hours. We have almost a thousand ships circling the planet pulling all who survived the first pulsar wave to safety."

"Pulsar?" someone shouted.

"Yes, a very powerful electromagnetic wave from a nearby star is what hit your planet ten days ago. All of you survived because you were protected in some fashion, either underground or behind thick steel walls."

Benny nodded, as did others around him. As he figured, the vault had saved him.

"How come you couldn't get here before the first wave?" one guy shouted.

"And who are you, anyway?" someone else shouted.

The man looked pained and Benny could see a deep sadness in his eyes. He clearly felt the loss of life as much as anyone.

"Let's just say I'm as human as the rest of you," the man said, "and from a very distant place. We were not able to save anyone or block the first pulsar wave, but we can save all of you who survived and let the second and final wave pass with no more deaths. Then you will all be put back on Earth to rebuild."

"What happens if we don't want to go back to that grave-yard?" one woman shouted.

A lot of people shouted "Yeah, what happens?"

Again the man smiled and said, "We'll come to that problem when the time comes. But for now, there is food and drink against the far wall and cots to take naps. There are showers for those of you who would like one, and fresh changes of clothes. This entire process will take about ten hours. Please relax and I will be back to talk with you as soon as I can. I have other rooms of survivors I must address."

"One last question," the professor beside me shouted at the man. "How many survived the first wave?"

"Worldwide," the man said, smiling, "almost two million. And we'll get them all, I promise."

As the noise of three hundred people talking at once filled

the room like a hard wave, Benny turned to David who had been talking about the aliens.

"Well, now what?"

"I have no idea," he said, his eyes wide.

At that moment, a girl's voice called out, "Professor," and Candice hit the professor's hug, sobbing.

Benny was glad to see she was still alive, but not as much as the boys in her class. She looked like she had gone through hell, and she smelled awful, like she had been sitting next to a dead body for days.

"Where have you been?" the professor asked, clearly fantastically glad to see her.

"At my apartment," she said between sobs.

That made sense. She had simply gone home to die beside her parents.

The owners of this big ship in orbit clearly were going to make sure that didn't happen.

At least not for the next ten hours.

CHAPTER 20

G ina was stunned. The man was more handsome in person than on her screens, if that was possible. And he had clearly been stunned when he saw her. But she had no idea how she was going to meet him.

But for the moment, that didn't matter. She had just under three hundred people in this big room she had to take care of. After Chairman Carson finished his introduction and left, she started to work.

First, she made sure the medical staff were dealing with as many of the injured and weak as possible. A good fifty people had just slumped to the floor when they arrived and looked to be in bad condition.

Medical had a few dozen smaller rooms set up to one side of the large room and forty of her people were moving the injured away.

Other ship members were spreading out food along one wall and still others were helping survivors to private showers.

A lot of people stood alone, just looking around, scared to death. Others had grouped up and were talking.

Gina made sure that she quickly had people talking with every solo person, moving them toward a group of other survivors if possible.

And Gina, at times, recorded her impressions of different people as she worked her way around the room. She was going to need to work with and try to help a large number of these people over the next few years. She was only one person and seeing everyone still in the city below packed into one room, it felt overwhelming to her.

And sad at the same time. The entire remaining population of a once great city now fit into one banquet room.

She pushed that thought away and went back to work. She knew that a large share of these people would not find a way to survive the summer. And that made her mad because she wanted to try to help everyone here.

But it became very clear as the medical staff moved more and more people away to smaller rooms that a lot of people just didn't want to be helped or survive.

She had never been a person who gave up on anything, but she couldn't imagine what the people in this room had gone through. It had impacted her and she had only been watching from a safe apartment in orbit.

When the rescue happened, the mass of people had been transported into the middle of the big room and they were now spreading out over the large space.

Many stood in front of the large screen showing the planet below. Many just found chairs and sat down, clearly too shocked or tired to even move.

As she walked around, giving orders, helping where she could, she noticed the dark-haired man from the big building often watched her. She was going to have to talk with him at some point.

He and his group were now all back together, and the girl seemed weak, but very happy to see them. Maybe she had decided she wanted to live after all.

Finally, after almost an hour, Gina moved over to the dark-haired man and the group with him from the big stone building. They were all munching on sandwiches and sipping what looked like a fruit drink of some kind. The dark-haired man and the two boys stood, the long-haired man sat and gave comfort to the young girl in the chair beside him.

Gina walked up, smiled, and stuck out her hand to the dark-haired man. "I'm Gina Helm," she said.

He smiled and took her hand. "Benny Slade."

He held her hand just a bit too long and she didn't mind at all. In fact, for a moment she got lost in his dark eyes and smile. And his touch sent shivers through her. She couldn't remember ever feeling like that about meeting anyone else.

When he finally released her hand, she felt a jolt of loss.

Wow, she was really going to have to get a grasp on herself.

Benny introduced her to the professor, the two teen-aged boys, and the young girl named Candice.

"It's very nice meeting you all," Gina said, reverting to her previous way of meeting and talking with survivors. "Is there anything I can get you while we wait to leave orbit?"

"How far are we going out?" the tall boy with red hair asked. She seemed to remember from the introduction that his name was David.

"About two light years," she said. "And we'll wait there until the next pulse passes and then come back. It will take about ten hours total."

"You have faster than light travel?" the other boy asked, clearly excited.

"It's called Trans-tunnel Drive," she said. "Nothing goes faster than light, but that drive bores a hole outside of space and allows long distances to be covered quickly."

"Wow," one of the boys said and she smiled.

This kind of discussion was relaxing her a little. She kept glancing up at Benny and he didn't say a word, just smiled.

"So where have you four been staying?" she asked.

At that question, Benny laughed. "You know the answer to that, don't you, since you found everyone on the island and brought them up here? I assume this is everyone on the island, and in other rooms are survivors from different areas. Right?"

She was stunned. She knew this man was smart from how he had set out to survive, but she didn't realize just how smart, and how calm he was in a situation that had most people just mumbling and afraid.

"You are all in the big stone building," she said, nodding and smiling at him. "And from what I can tell, you are pretty set up for surviving the summer. Well done."

Damn those eyes of his were amazing as he stared at her and nodded.

"So why do you speak English?" the professor asked.

"Actually," she said, "we are all speaking a form of what is called Standard, but when you were transported, we gave you all the ability to understand and speak Standard. It will always sound like we are talking in the same language. But I speak English just fine as well."

"So where exactly are you from?" Benny asked.

She laughed. "Hard to explain."

Benny pointed to the two boys. "I'm sure these two will understand, so give it a try."

She nodded, doing her best to not stare into his eyes too much. "My home world circles a planet in the Lesser Magenelic Cloud."

Both boys reacted at once, excited. "That's a satellite galaxy of the Milky Way," David said to Benny.

"It's a very, very long ways away," the other boy said.

"Are there aliens there?"

She shook her head. "There are no alien civilizations at all in this galaxy or in many others that have been seeded with human life. Only humans like us."

"So this is your real form?" David asked. "Not some sort of image?"

"Everyone on this ship is human," she said, smiling at the young man. "I am very real. The ship is called *Star Conscious* and has a crew of about two thousand, including families, all from human worlds spread over four or five galaxies."

Now even Benny seemed a little shocked, but he said nothing, so she took that as a good moment to move on. Even though she really wanted to stay here, she had a job to do.

"I have to keep moving and checking on everyone," she said. "But I will be back to talk more shortly."

"Looking forward to it," Benny said, smiling a half-smile at her.

Damn, it was everything she could do to just walk away without looking back. Luckily, not more than twenty steps away was another group she hadn't talked to.

And a minute later, when she glanced back, Benny was still watching her as she had watched him the last few days.

CHAPTER 21

B enny had no idea how the hundreds of other people in the room felt, but after the little speech by some man in charge, he kept verging on sheer panic that came close to cutting through the trained calm in his head.

He made himself focus on what was happening around him as people spread out, some going for food, others being helped by medical staff, others moving for showers and fresh clothing.

He asked Candice if she needed any medical help and she just shook her head. "Just some food and something to drink."

The professor found her a chair and one for himself after he sent the boys off to get them all something to eat.

In the big room, the five of them were closer to the big window or view screen showing the planet below than most others. After the first few minutes, most everyone had moved more into the big room or to the far walls.

The woman that had shocked him when he saw her with

his attraction for her was clearly someone in charge. She was working her way around the room, talking with survivors, getting some of them help, sending someone for food for others.

More than likely, these survivors, probably all from Manhattan, were her responsibility.

And if he had to guess, she had been studying everyone ahead of time. That's how he would set it up if he knew this was coming.

As he watched her, he became more and more attracted to her. She was clearly in shape, strong, and moved like an athlete.

And she was smart, in control, and smiled easily, even under these circumstances.

The boys got back with the food. He took what looked like a roast beef sandwich and a bottle of orange fruit juice that tasted wonderful.

As they ate and he watched the black-haired woman, David asked the professor, "Why the question about the number of survivors?"

"Because there is a magic number of humans that it takes to build a population," the professor said between bites and encouraging Candice to eat slowly. "The human race, at least on this planet, would need population to survive and have a large enough gene pool to make the effort even worthwhile."

"And you know this how?" Benny asked.

"It's my field," he said, smiling. "Or it used to be."

"Is two million enough?" David asked.

The professor laughed. "Far, far more than enough."

Benny figured that at least that was good to hear.

Then, like a shining light in the darkness, the woman with short black hair walked toward them and stuck out her hand, saying her name was Gina Helm.

In all his years, Benny had never felt a touch so electric, a look so attractive as hers.

Up close she was even better looking than she had been from across the room. Her eyes were a deep green and just seemed to see everything about him.

He flat didn't want to let go of her hand, but managed to and then introduced her to the others.

They talked for a far too short a time before she excused herself to move on. Clearly she had been watching everyone in this room for days ahead, and was the person in charge.

After she moved on to the next group, Benny moved slightly so he could watch her and then asked David a question. "Can you explain to me what she meant when she described where she was from?"

"There are billions of stars in this galaxy, most would have planets," David said.

"But not all would hold human life like Earth," Freddy said, "But at least hundreds of millions would be able to."

"Think of this galaxy like the sun and there are other smaller galaxies circling it like planets," David said.

"She is from one of those other galaxies," Freddy said. "And she said that the crew on this ship is all human from thousands of worlds."

Benny shook his head, not even slightly capable of understanding what the two boys were saying. "So she's from another planet?"

"Yes," David said, "One so far away it's impossible to imagine traveling that distance."

"So she's an alien?" Benny asked.

David and Freddy both shook their heads. "There has always been a theory that humans didn't originate on this planet, that we were seeded by other more advanced humans. That's what she said, so she would be as human as we are."

"Looks human," the professor said, smiling at Benny.

Benny laughed. "That she does."

A voice came over a speaker system, saying simply over the noise. "Everyone is on board safely. We are moving to a safe point now."

David pointed to the window.

Benny pulled his gaze from Gina and turned just in time to see the planet shrink and then vanish in a blur of gray motion.

Maybe ten seconds later the stars returned, with no planet.

"Wow," David said, clearly excited. "It took only a few seconds to move two light years."

Benny had no real idea how far it was they had just traveled. And he honestly wasn't sure if he wanted to know. He had enough to deal with at the moment.

CHAPTER 22

Gina moved slowly around the room for the next hour, glancing over at Benny at times and once smiling at him and he smiled back.

Now, after almost two hours, the room was settled and her staff had a pretty good control of all the situations.

The room's disinfectant air cleaners had also cleared most of the smells as well, which she was thankful for. In short order, she would be living in that smell of death. She was glad it was gone for the moment now.

Finally, she found herself just standing, looking around. Everything for all the people seemed to be in control.

So she turned and worked her way back toward Benny and the others from the big stone building.

"Looks like the situation is under control," Benny said, smiling at her as she approached. "Nice job."

"Control might be the wrong term," she said, smiling back. "Call it contained panic."

Benny kept smiling and she was drawn even more to him and that wonderful smile that actually reached his eyes. "Been fighting that myself a lot over the last ten days."

"Can't say that I blame you," she said. She looked away from Benny and at the young girl. "You feeling better?"

Candice nodded, but said nothing, just stayed leaning against the professor.

The professor nodded his thanks to her. Clearly he was doing fine as well, taking the responsibility of his last class very seriously. She liked that about him.

"You boys doing all right?" she asked the other two.

Both nodded. "Can't believe we're two light years from Earth."

"It took only seconds," the second one said.

She smiled. "Distance in space between stars is vast. So even at the speed we took this jump, it takes a long time to get some places."

David nodded. "Like to your home world."

"Yes," she said, nodding. "That's a great distance away."

"So what does your home world look like?" Benny asked.

She looked into his eyes and smiled. "Actually, very similar to yours, except that it has a little more land mass and a little less water. But I was born in a city on an island very similar to your Manhattan Island."

All of them nodded and she was about to excuse herself again to keep making rounds when Benny asked a very simple question. "So you sticking around after this rescue operation?"

"I am," she said, figuring it wouldn't hurt to tell him since he would never remember anyway. "Thousands of us will be embedding on your planet to help the recovery along."

"It would be great having you in our building," David said.

Benny smiled at her and nodded.

"I just might take you up on that if you'll have me."

"I think we have more than enough room," the professor said. But he was frowning. She didn't want him to ask the next question. Clearly the professor was very smart as well. No wonder he and Benny had made such a good team getting that big building cleared and set up for survival.

"I've got to go check on everyone else," she said, smiling at the professor and Candice, then at Benny.

His gaze was intense and she had a hunch he also realized something about what she said was wrong.

"Back in a short time," she said, lightly touching his arm as she walked past.

And that simple touch had sent a shock wave through her.

What in the world was going on?

Forcing herself to not look back again at Benny, she started another slow circuit of the big room. She really, really wanted to get to know him. More than anyone she had met before.

But that would happen once she reached the planet.

Nothing that happened here in the next few hours would make a difference because he wouldn't remember it.

CHAPTER 23

Benny watched her go, wishing he could just walk along with her and talk with her and stay close to her.

Then he glanced down at the professor. "Did something just happen there that I missed?"

Benny had a hunch he knew what it was, but he wanted the professor to confirm his suspicions.

"She's going to come to live in our building," the professor said.

"That is so cool," David said.

"But we won't remember any of this," the professor said, making an assumption that had not yet been stated.

Benny nodded and glanced at where Gina knelt talking with two survivors sitting in chairs.

The professor was right, Benny was sure. He was going to have to meet her all over again.

Part of him was sad about that and part of him was excited that he wouldn't remember any of this.

"We don't ask her that question," Benny said to everyone.

"No point anyway if you are right," David said. "We won't remember the answer."

"But we will meet her again," the professor said. "And even if we don't remember, she's going to be a great help."

Benny couldn't agree more.

Over the next few hours the professor managed to get more food and drink into Candice to make her stronger and want to come back to the building. But through that smell on a hot day was going to be a very nasty hike for her. Benny wasn't sure if she could make it.

But he had a hunch that if Gina showed up, she would work with them to find Candice and others to join the building, and that was exactly what they needed.

She would remember and she would know exactly where everyone was located.

She came by and talked with them twice more in the next few hours and the boys asked her all kinds of science fiction questions. Mostly Benny just listened and enjoyed the time being close to her.

Sometime after nine hours, true to his word, the man who had given the speech at first came back in and everyone got quiet.

"Everyone on the planet, almost two million souls, has survived the second and final wave of deadly electromagnet waves," he said.

The room gave him a cheer and a lot shouted out "Thank you!"

Benny did the same.

And across the room he could see that Gina looked relieved. Benny had no doubt that saving over two million people had to have been a massive undertaking. More than he wanted to imagine.

His style was helping one person at a time.

"We are returning to Earth," the man said, "and will be in Earth orbit in a minute or so."

"So do we have an option of going to another planet?" someone shouted.

"No," the man said, which caused the room to explode in talking.

The man held up his hand for silence and got it. "We will take the extremely wounded and the near-death sick, but all of you, and the two million others on all the ships are the future of humanity on Earth. We can't rob Earth of that."

"How do we survive?" someone shouted from behind where Benny stood.

"Some of you won't," the man said bluntly. "But many will, enough to rebuild a wonderful culture and society and preserve much of what is already there. Your job is to save the old art and culture and build new on top of it."

"Wow, the guy is blunt," David said. "And guys, we are back in orbit."

Benny glanced around to see the planet below them.

Suddenly, beside Benny the professor shouted out, "We won't remember any of this, will we?"

The officer smiled. "It is possible, but unlikely," he said. "Most of you won't remember any of this."

That stunned everyone even more than the death sentence he had just declared on many people in the room.

Benny smiled at Gina and pretended to tip his hat at her in thanks.

She smiled back and nodded.

"I wish each and every one of you luck," the man said. "The future of the human race on the planet Earth depends on all of you."

With that a shimmering wave swept over the room.

Benny knew he was going home, to the city he loved, and his new home near the top of the Empire State Building.

CHAPTER 24

Gina watched as they all vanished, leaving only her and her team scattered around the room.

Everyone stood in silence for a moment, then turned silently to start cleaning up. Everyone had prepared for this rescue for a long time. It was now over and her job and the others embedding into the culture was just starting.

"Great job," Chairman Carson said to her, stepping down off the stage. He was the captain of this ship. Since every Seeder ship was a business to itself and everyone on board was paid, the captain was called Chairman.

"Thank you," she said. "I'll be starting the next stage tomorrow."

The Chairman nodded, his normally happy face drawn with lines of exhaustion. She hadn't seen him look so tired before.

"We'll cloak in a week or so," he said, "so local sector rescue ships won't know we are remaining here. Get some rest before you start. At this point, the deadline is past, the long slow job of helping rebuild this civilization starts."

"I'm feeling that," she said, nodding. "But also excited to get down there to help and save as many as I can."

He nodded. "Anything you need, don't hesitate."

"Thank you, Chairman."

He transported away, leaving her standing and staring at the mess where over two hundred survivors had been a short time before. The two empty chairs where the professor and Candice had sat seemed hauntingly alone.

She needed to get Candice back to the big building first. Of that she had no doubt.

And she really wanted to meet Benny again, and have time to actually get to know him this time around.

She spent the next hour working with her crew and the medical staff on those injured survivors they had not sent back. There were almost forty of them and she knew they would all be transferred to another ship to be taken to worlds that had volunteered to take them as refugees. Most of the survivors would survive and would get mental help as well as the medical.

Finally, she went back to her apartment, took a long shower, got something to eat, and then went to her screens to check on the people on the island.

No one was moving. It was late afternoon and more than likely the day was hot.

She focused down on the man she had met and was so attracted to. Benny sat in his apartment, alone, his feet up, staring out over the city. He had made a former office into an apartment and it looked very comfortable. He had even set up a nice kitchen with a dining table near a window for the view.

She had no idea what he was thinking about, and she wished she was there to ask him.

Then, as she watched, he did something she couldn't believe he could do.

He stood up, went over to a pad of yellow paper on a counter, then in large script he wrote a note.

As she stared at it, she just shook her head.

The note said:

Gina, please get Candice on your way here tomorrow.

He held that up to the sky for a moment, then put it on the table in plain view.

Then he wrote another note.

I'll set you up an apartment.
There are a lot of people we need to save when you get here.

He put that note on the table beside the first one and then smiled upward before moving over to the chair to sit down again and put his feet up.

He remembered!

Gina just stared at the screen and the slight smile on Benny's face.

How in the hell had he remembered?

How was that even possible?

She just stared at that smile on his handsome face and then just started laughing.

She had some research to do and do quickly.

She teleported to the transportation department of the ship.

Seeders could just teleport from place to place within reason, but every ship also had a transport department for moving others and supplies. And that department had been responsible for the smooth transport of all the survivors who came to this ship. She needed one question answered before she did anything.

She needed to know how Benny could remember.

She needed to know if it was a glitch, or if there was something, as she suspected, very, very special about Benny Slade.

Besides the fact that all she wanted to do was jump him and make love to him.

CHAPTER 25

Benny awoke with a slight headache in his big bed. The sun was high in the sky and he glanced at a clock he had put beside the bed. It was after two in the afternoon.

Ten hours.

Then he bolted upright in bed, sitting there, trying to calm his racing heart.

He had had a dream about being taken up to a ship and meeting the most stunning woman he could ever imagine.

In his dream, he had been taken from sleep right before sunrise, about 4:30 a.m. and his dream had him, and everyone, being on the ship for almost ten hours.

He kept staring at the clock.

How was that possible?

He dropped back onto the bed, staring up at the tile in the

former office ceiling. They had said no one would remember. Had he imagined it all?

Had he imagined Gina Helm?

He hoped not, but his racing heart wanted to let him believe he had.

He had never given much thought to people living on other planets. The very idea of it had never interested him much at all, actually.

Now it seemed people on a lot of other planets were a very real thing.

Or he had just dreamed it all.

Far more likely.

But not once in his life had he slept for seventeen hours, which was how long it had been since he had crawled into bed.

He lay there in his bed until finally he couldn't stay still any longer.

He had to move, see if there were any answers.

He took a long shower, got into fresh clothes, and headed down to a public area where the professor and the boys spent their time. It was near all their rooms and they all ate lunches and dinners together.

All three of them were sitting there, not talking.

"Anyone have any idea why we all slept so late?" Benny asked, grabbing a cold glass of iced tea and sitting down with them.

"Not a clue," the professor said. "Never slept that long in my entire life."

"We all did," David said. "I think the planet got hit with something again and this time only knocked us out."

Freddy shook his head. "Aliens, I'm sure. They wanted to plant trackers on us or something for their experiments."

Both David and the professor shook their heads.

"It was sure weird," Benny said.

They talked for a few more minutes, then Benny decided to take some action. He had a hunch, if his dream was true, they were going to start having company fairly quickly.

"I'm going to spend the evening setting up a second apartment on my floor. I think because of our lights at night, we need to start getting ready for company pretty soon."

They divided up work, including helping him bring up a second bed, some furniture from an office ten floors down, and another dining table from a lunch room even more floors down. To move furniture, they used the service elevator and he hated it. Even knowing how to get himself out of the elevator didn't help. Having an elevator powered by a generator just wasn't his idea of a confidence builder.

There were two large bathrooms with showers on his floor, so it would easily divide into an apartment for Gina.

He hoped she would want it.

He hoped she was real.

If not, he was going to a lot of work to make a living apartment for a figment of his imagination.

He headed back up to his own apartment after a half hour to sit and do some planning while the professor and the boys did chores and made sure the generators were all working fine, as well as the alarms for the monitors on the doors.

Then after dinner, they would actually set up the new apartment.

It was as he sat looking out over the city that he got the feeling he was being watched.

The windows were tinted to not allow anyone to see in, so he knew it wasn't coming from outside.

The woman of his dreams had tuned in again.

If she was real, and believed he wouldn't remember, she was in for a shock.

He smiled and went over to the table and wrote a couple of notes for her in very large letters.

If she was watching, that would really mess with her mind, and that made him smile even more.

If she wasn't watching, if she didn't really exist, then he hoped one of the survivors they ran across was a good trained counselor, because he was going to need real help for believing in a dream woman from space.

THE FIRST STEPS

CHAPTER 26

Gina had spent a good hour with the fine people in the transport area, trying to understand why anyone from the surface would remember their time on the ship.

She was told there were only two reasons. One was that the equipment had malfunctioned slightly, but she was assured that hadn't happened after they spent a good thirty minutes checking everything over.

The second reason was that the person had the Seeder gene. That tended to sometimes block such things as mind erase. Not all the time, but sometimes, if the person had a very, very strong Seeder gene.

She hadn't known until that moment that there was anything like a Seeder gene. But it seemed there was, and it was a prerequisite to joining the Seeders. It allowed Seeders to comprehend vast amounts of information and not forget any of it over hundreds or even thousands of years of life.

And with the right treatment, it allowed the person to live basically forever, barring accidents. Having that gene allowed the health treatments that stopped all aging and sickness in all Seeders.

So Benny Slade had the Seeder gene.

The idea of that stunned her even more than she wanted to think about.

After her hour with the transportation department, she sent a message to the Chairman that she needed to talk with him.

She wanted to know what was allowed with survivors who remembered the rescue and what wasn't. Not a question ever covered in the training up to this mission, because no one had been expected to remember.

"My office now," was all he responded.

She jumped to his office. It was large, with a number of chairs and a large couch. The walls were a light tan and covered with photos from different planets. There was a large wooden desk with hidden screens that she knew floated over the desk when in use.

She had only been in his office once before and felt she liked Chairman Carson more because of the informal nature of the room.

She was stunned that he had a visitor.

The man with the chairman stood about six feet tall and had long gray hair flowing down his back that he had pulled into a ponytail. He was imposing and striking at the same time. He flat radiated power from his dark eyes.

Chairman Carson was standing in front of his desk talking with the man as she arrived. Carson turned to her. "Gina Helm, I would like you to meet Chairman Wade Ray."

She managed to say, "Nice meeting you."

And then she shook his hand before her tired mind realized that the man she was meeting was one of the most powerful and oldest of all Seeders. No one really knew how old he was. Or even what galaxy he was born in.

What was he doing here?

"Sorry to interrupt," she managed to choke out.

Chairman Ray just smiled. "We were actually talking about you and the great job you did. And about one of the survivors in your area."

Gina managed to get her thoughts back together and said simply, "Benny Slade?"

"You met him I understand," Chairman Ray said, his eyes intense.

"I met him and talked with him a number of times," Gina said, "and found him really amazing and very smart. And I discovered that he did not have his memory wiped by the transport."

"He wouldn't be wiped," Chairman Ray said, and Chairman Carson nodded. "How did you discover this?"

"I checked in on him about an hour ago," she said, "and he must have sensed me watching him and wrote me a note, asked me to pick up another survivor when I arrived in the morning."

"Wow," Chairman Carson said. "And you came here to tell me that?"

Gina shook her head. "Actually, I came here to ask if I could recruit him as a Seeder in this mission. He would be valuable help if I didn't have to hide from him."

Chairman Ray smiled and nodded. "See if you can convince him to join you."

Then Ray turned to Chairman Carson. "Let me know if he does join us."

Chairman Ray then turned to face Gina with those intense eyes of his. "Great job with all this and for discovering Benny Slade's presence in your group. Good luck on the coming mission. I am sure I'll be seeing you soon."

With a slight smile, he vanished.

She stood shocked for a moment, then turned to Chairman Carson. "Can you explain to me what that was all about?"

Carson shrugged and pulled up the image on a screen on his wall of her talking with Benny Slade in the big room. "Somehow he knew about this Benny person and asked about him and your reaction with Benny Slade. So we watched your interaction with Benny and then you asked to see me."

"So why does a survivor on a very damaged planet interest Chairman Ray?" Gina asked, her tired mind swimming in confusion.

Chairman Carson went around the desk and dropped into his big chair and let out a long sigh. "When you figure that out, please let me know as well."

CHAPTER 27

That evening after dinner, Benny and the professor and the two boys sat up Gina Helm's apartment on the opposite side of the same floor that Benny was on. There were two office doors and a foyer between the two apartments.

Benny didn't tell them who was coming because he was starting to think he imagined it all. But even so, he wanted the apartment to be clean and comfortable.

They moved in a large flat screen and tan living room furniture and a library of old movies. They set up a large bed and turned a small office into a closet with a bench next to where the bed was.

They also managed to move up a fridge and set it up near a sink in a small glassed-in break room, leaving the table and chairs and the dishes in the cabinets. The room already had a small microwave and hot plate, so it would work pretty well, as far as Benny was concerned. Not as nice as his kitchen on the other side of the floor, but good enough.

Then they set up a generator to run on the balcony outside of the apartment, so both of the apartments on the floor could have their own power and air-conditioning.

They got it running to cool down the apartment.

Every so often he got the sense that Gina was watching him and he would glance up and give her the thumbs-up signal. He hoped she would like the place.

And he really hoped she saw his note about picking up Candice on the way here.

Actually, he hoped more than anything that she was real.

After they were done, the professor and the boys went back downstairs to watch a movie. Once again Benny stretched out in his living room, his lights low so he could see out over the darkening city.

There were a few lights scattered over the dark city, but not many.

And he knew people out there could see his lights here as well.

If he hadn't just imagined everything about Gina, very soon they would be recruiting more and more people to join them and help with survival.

And if Gina was real, he had about a thousand questions to ask her, not only about her job and people and space, but about herself.

He really, really wanted to get to know her better.

A lot better.

And never once in his life had he felt that way about a figment of his imagination.

He managed to doze off in his chair after an hour or so and crawl into bed by ten with the alarm set for five a.m. He wanted to be downstairs to greet Gina and Candice.

He had a hunch she would start early, in the coolness of the morning.

That's what he would do.

CHAPTER 28

Benny was just crawling out of bed when Gina took one last look at her screens, made sure she had what she needed in her light pack, including water, and informed transport she would be leaving the ship shortly.

She wore jeans and a light white blouse with a sports bra under it. She had on tennis shoes and had three changes of clothes and a pair of running shoes protected from the smell in a sealed bag.

She wore nose filters against the smell for herself and carried a gas mask from the city below for Candice. But she knew that wouldn't begin to stop the odor of walking past and over thousands of dead bodies decomposing in the heat of the streets.

It was not going to be a pretty sight, and she hoped Candice had the stomach for it. If the girl fainted, Gina would transport them both closer to the big stone building that was their destination.

She might have to do that anyway if Candice was passed out. Or if Candice couldn't walk, she would just drug her and transport them both.

Gina did one more double-check of her light provisions. She could transport back to this apartment at any time, but better that she was prepared to stay on the surface as much as possible.

She took a deep breath and then said to herself, "Here we go."

A moment later she found herself in the dim apartment where Candice had been hiding. The decomposing smell of human flesh hit her hard and she forced herself to breathe through her nose to let the filters hold the smell down some.

She moved down the hallway to where Candice had been staying in her bedroom. The girl was curled up under the blankets.

"Candice," Gina said softly. "We need to get out of here and back to the big building with your friends."

"Who are you?" Candice asked weakly, looking up at her.

"I'm just a friend," Gina said. "Come on, let's get you back to the professor and your friends."

"You can take me there?" Candice asked, but didn't move.

"I can," Gina said. She tried to help Candice up, but the young girl just wasn't there. Her arms felt like limp sacks of flesh. There was no doubt to Gina that Candice wasn't going to be able to walk the fifteen blocks to the big stone building.

Especially through all the death.

Gina eased a sedative out of her pack and brushed it over Candice's face as if she was brushing the girl's filthy hair out of her face.

Candice slumped out cold almost instantly.

Gina put the gas mask on Candice's face, then put one arm under the young girl's shoulders and the other under her thighs and lifted her. Candice didn't weigh that much.

Gina then jumped to a spot she knew was blind to Benny's cameras about a half block away from the big stone building and around a corner.

The smell on the street was ten times worse than it had been in the apartment and it made her stagger.

She had imagined this to be bad, but nothing like this.

And the bodies around her were bloated and ugly colors and didn't look anything close to human anymore.

Her stomach threatened to rebel, but she managed to control that by looking up at a wall and focusing on a fire escape there.

Then she forced herself to breathe only through her nose, but the smell made her eyes water and she wanted to just stop and throw up.

She moved around the corner so Benny's security cameras could see her and then leaned against the side of a building for a moment, still holding Candice in her arms.

The feel of the solid stone building wall gave her strength.

This was going to be so much harder than she had ever imagined.

After a moment she started forward, making sure to walk mostly in the street around the cars because that was far, far easier than walking around the bodies she didn't want to look at on the sidewalk.

When she was within a hundred paces of the main door to the big stone building, it flew open and both Benny and the professor came charging out, moving as fast as they could into the street.

"Got her," Benny said, smiling at Gina and taking Candice.

The professor moved around and supported Gina and the four of them headed into the building.

"I'm fine," Gina said. "And I think she is as well. She just fainted."

"Professor, get the doors locked back up and the alarms reset," Benny said. "We'll take her to the floor below yours for cleanup and such."

Benny got onto an elevator carrying Candice and Gina followed.

"Glad I wasn't dreaming," Benny said as the door closed and they started up.

Gina smiled at him. "Glad you weren't either."

Then all the way up they just stared at each other, smiling like kids on a first date.

CHAPTER 29

O n the excuse of looking at their security set-up, Benny had the professor go down to the lower levels with him. Benny had a hunch that if he hadn't imagined Gina, and she had seen his note, she and Candice would be arriving in the next half hour or so, before the sun really climbed into the sky and started to heat up the mess outside once again.

The lower levels had a faint smell of rotting death, but the solid building was holding most of it out. But Benny had no doubt it was going to be a long, hot, stinking summer.

As Benny and the professor reached the security room, an alarm sounded and there, on the screen, Gina staggered around the edge of a building about a block from their main doors and leaned against a wall.

She was real!

Spaceships and rescues and millions of survivors were all real.

Holy shit! How was that possible?

But it was.

He just stared at the screen, his mouth open, every muscle in his body frozen.

Gina Helm, a human from a very great distance away, stood there on the corner with Candice in her arms.

Gina had the exact same short black hair that he remembered, and the trim body now dressed in jeans and a light blouse. She looked just as she did on the spaceship in orbit.

She was real!

It had not been a dream.

Gina rested for a moment against the building, then went into the street and started toward the main door, seemingly carrying Candice without much of a problem.

"That's Candice!" the professor shouted.

That shocked Benny into movement and the two of them took off running down the two flights of stairs and to the front door. Benny got it open and they both ran out into the intense stink of the street as Gina got close.

He smiled at Gina, not at all believing his eyes.

Then he took Candice from Gina's arms.

Candice was so light, it shocked him.

As the professor locked up, he and Gina took Candice up the elevator to the floor under where the professor and the boys lived. It had once been a number of small offices, each with bathrooms. The room had a large main area just off the elevators. They had set up that floor with showers, trash disposal for clothes that could not be salvaged from the smell, and soaking sinks near some wash machines for the clothing that could be saved.

They had also brought in about forty bathrobes of all sizes and had them hanging around the area. No one was allowed onto the living floors smelling like the death in the streets. That was the rule of the building and an important one.

He put Candice on a tabletop near the center of the big area and checked her vitals. She seemed to just be sleeping.

"I had to knock her out with a light sedative," Gina said. "She should be fine in a few hours and some food."

"Good," Benny said. "Very glad you saw my note."

"And that note was very good thinking on your part," she said. "It forced me to research and learn a lot about why you could remember the ship."

"I'm interested in hearing about that," Benny said, smiling at her.

As the elevator dinged and the professor came bounding into the room, Gina turned and introduced herself, using the same name she had used on the ship.

Benny figured that was her real name, but he would ask later to make sure.

She told the professor she had seen Candice trying to make her way here and just helped her. Benny nodded to her in agreement of her cover story as she turned back.

"You have showers here?" Gina asked, looking around.

Benny showed her the set-up of the different offices, all with bathrooms and installed showers that they had put in, while the professor stayed close to Candice.

"You bring a change of clothes?" Benny asked her.

"Got some in sealed bags in my pack," she said. "And my pack can be wiped down and won't absorb odors. How about I get myself and Candice showered and cleaned up and into fresh clothes? What do I do with her old clothes?"

Benny showed her the black bags to wrap them up in and where to throw them down an elevator shaft they had blocked open.

He was stunned at how calm she was acting and sounding. His heart was racing a mile a minute and it was everything he could do to stay calm.

The attraction he felt for her was more now than it had been on the ship.

"You should be able to save your clothes," he said. "Toss them in a sink for them to soak and I'll show you how to wash them later."

"Thank you," she said, nodding.

Then she looked into his eyes and both of them sort of froze.

Finally he managed to say, "We have a lot of talking to do later."

"With that I agree," she said, smiling at him and making the breath in his throat catch. "About more than you can ever imagine."

CHAPTER 30

Gina waited with Candice while Benny and the professor took showers, changed clothes, and tossed their other clothes into some hot water to soak. Then they headed upstairs, leaving her to help the young girl.

She was stunned at how handsome Benny was coming out of that room with fresh clothes and wet hair. She just wanted to touch him. And that was so out of character for her.

"We'll be at the top of that flight of stairs if you need help with Candice," Benny said as they left.

"I'll manage fine and bring her up with me," Gina said.

Then she stripped Candice and tossed her clothes away. Then Gina took off her clothes as well and put them in a sink full of water next to Benny's clothes to soak.

Then she picked up Candice and carried her to a shower in a side office.

Candice didn't wake up, which was fine. Gina got both of them scrubbed down and both of their hair cleaned. She used some of the special chemicals she had brought from the ship to neutralize the odor. She dried them both off and got Candice in underwear and a bathrobe.

Then Gina pulled out one of her extra pair of clothes, took her nose plug filters out, and stored them in her pack, and got dressed.

Then she wiped her pack down and put it over her shoulder.

"Time to go the final steps to home," she said to Candice as she picked her up.

The young girl was so light, it was scary. She carried Candice up the flight of stairs without a problem.

It felt good to actually be rescuing someone from certain death. She knew that they had rescued everyone on the planet, but that had only been for a few hours.

This rescue of Candice, Gina hoped, would last, and that Candice would help rebuild this new world. All over the planet a thousand Seeders were doing the same thing, trying to help one person at a time to survive.

When she reached the next floor, Benny, the professor, and the two young men were there.

Benny quickly took Candice from Gina and got the young girl into a bed in a private room off to one side of the main room.

The professor had fixed some soup and had some crackers. The two boys just hovered close by, looking relieved and worried for their friend.

After Benny got Candice tucked in, he came out. "Take turns sitting with her and get her food and water when she wakes up," he said to the professor and the boys.

Gina then introduced herself to the two boys and both of them thanked her for bringing Candice.

After a short time, Benny said in front of everyone, "We have an apartment you might like that we just finished, if you are interested in staying with us for a while."

He smiled at her and she nodded. "I think I would like that. There are a lot of things I can do to help out."

"We'll talk about that tonight over dinner," Benny said, smiling at her.

Damn that smile of his could melt an iceberg. And she was far, far from being an iceberg.

She and Benny climbed up the flights of stairs so he could show her the apartment they had set up for her. They didn't really talk. She wasn't sure what exactly to say yet. It slightly annoyed her that she was acting like a school girl with a crush on a guy, but everything about Benny affected her and she had no idea why.

But she liked the feeling of really being attracted to someone. It had been a long time since that had happened and never this strong on first sight that she could remember.

She left her pack in her new bedroom. She was going to like staying here. The apartment, even being put together from what had clearly been an office area, was comfortable and the view was something to behold.

The windows in her living room showed an amazing city stretching far beyond the limits of the water on either side of the island. What had happened to this planet was one of the great tragedies of the galaxy. Of that she had no doubt.

She walked slowly around, looking at all the details Benny had set up for her as he quickly described it all. Granted, she had watched them set up this apartment, but actually being in it felt different.

It felt right.

"This is wonderful," she said after Benny was done with the short tour. "It seems perfect."

She smiled at him and he just looked into her eyes for a long moment.

"Thanks," he said, finally. "Not as good as your place on the ship, I bet."

"In some ways," she said, "I think it's better."

She wanted to add that it was better because he was close by, but she didn't. She was amazingly attracted to this man, but she really didn't know him at all. They both had so much to learn about each other.

She had to be careful, not move too fast, even though she wanted to.

Actually, what she wanted more than anything was to just kiss him and pull him to that freshly made bed.

But she managed to remain in control.

And she had no idea how she was going to tell him about the Seeder part of things.

"How about we go down and check on the professor and the boys and Candice," Benny said after a moment of silence. "Grab a little lunch, then bring it back up here and talk."

"That sounds perfect," she said.

And it did.

CHAPTER 31

Benny checked on Candice, who still seemed to be sleeping comfortably. The professor and the boys were not going to be far from her. He hadn't realized how much her disappearance had really bothered them until Candice showed up on the ship.

Now it seemed her appearance had given them new life. They had set up a chair just inside her open bedroom door so someone would be there when she woke up.

When he came out, the professor and David were sitting at the big oak meeting table they used to eat meals and Freddy was sitting just inside Candice's door listening to their conversation.

Gina was standing, leaning against a counter so she could face everyone. And it felt wonderful to have her here and part of this group.

It actually felt natural, which was odd considering she had

only been here an hour or so at most.

He dug out of the fridge the fixings for sandwiches and started to put them together.

"I think we need to be getting a few more floors ready for more guests," he said as he worked. He was using some of the last thinly-sliced roast beef from the deli that they had kept in the freezer. He was going to miss deli roast beef more than he wanted to think about.

And bread. He and the professor had talked at one point about trying to figure out how to make bread and grow vegetables and other things, but at the moment, with canned food and other things that didn't spoil quickly, they had more than enough to make it for a year or so. It just wasn't going to be a varied diet, but it would keep them alive.

"How many people are you set up for now?" Gina asked.

"We could hold fifty, maybe," the professor said and Benny nodded his agreement. "We're ready for that now."

But with fifty, Benny knew that would make it critical to go out regularly searching for more food.

"That's a pretty good number," Gina said, nodding.

From what Benny could tell, she was impressed.

David and the professor then asked Gina some basic questions and she had told them she had been in the subway when everything happened, had holed up down there for a time, but decided she didn't like that and it felt dangerous. Plus she said it smelled bad down there, with the moisture and all. So she came up to see if she could find anyone alive.

Benny had just listened to her cover story, nodding. It was sound and had no places for any real questions.

"Where you from originally?" the professor asked.

"My family moved around a lot," she said. "And I just kept on moving when I got older. So nowhere, really. But I sure love New York."

Benny smiled and nodded. Again a great cover story that didn't pin her to any one place. There was absolutely nothing at all suspicious about her story and if he didn't remember meeting her on a huge spaceship in orbit, he would have been completely buying the story as well.

"You can see your lights from all over the city," Gina said. "So as more discover they are not in a good place, they will try to get here, I'm sure. So I agree with Benny that setting up more living quarters would be a good idea. But fifty is a great start."

"You think we should track some of their lights as well and try to offer them a room here?" the professor asked.

"I don't think it would hurt," Benny said, putting the sandwiches in front of everyone and handing Gina a plate. Then he took Freddy a plate with a sandwich on it and a small bag of potato chips.

The professor nodded. "I agree. After Candice wakes up, I'll start really looking at more spaces in the building we could convert easily."

Benny nodded. "Gina and I will be upstairs. I want her to fill me in on what she's seen around the city. Let us know when Candice wakes."

"We will," the professor said, nodding.

When they got into the stairwell and started the climb, both carrying their plates of food, Gina looked over at Benny. "Those are some very good people you have there."

"I know," he said. "And all three of them are as smart as a whip."

She laughed. "Never heard that expression before."

"I'm not surprised," Benny said. "It's an old one."

And he wasn't surprised. No way anyone just studying the planet could learn all the language. So he figured that the walk up the stairs was as good a time as any to ask the first of what he figured would be a thousand or more questions.

"How long did you have to study this planet, anyway?"

"Basic preparations I did on the way here three weeks ago," she said. "But almost all of what I studied was in the last ten days."

"Wow, you really didn't have any time, did you?"

She sighed beside him and he looked over at her pained face.

"I think if the powers that be out there in the big universe had learned of this tragedy sooner," she said, softly, "they would have saved a lot more people than just the two million from the last wave."

She was actually pained by what had happened here. This planet, this city, wasn't just her job. These were real people to her and to those she worked for.

That was very clear.

And at that moment he realized just how important saving lives was to Gina and her people. And that eased about a thousand of his fears.

There were still a few thousand more he could think of, but his feelings for her eased a lot of them as well.

CHAPTER 32

G ina couldn't remember when she enjoyed a lunch more than that first one with Benny. They sat at his table in his apartment near the windows looking out over the city. The air-conditioning was running softly in the background and she could faintly hear the generator on the balcony outside.

The city spread out around them still looked fresh and almost alive. From where they were, they couldn't see any of the streets and that was fine with her. She didn't need a constant reminder of what was below them.

They talked about everything as they ate, from Benny's degrees in college, which didn't really surprise her that he was that smart, to her home planet and how she had grown up and been recruited into the Seeders.

And the sandwich had been amazing. She ended up devouring it and then telling him how much she liked it.

"Don't get used to it," he said, looking sad. "Not a lot of that beef left and there won't be more for a very long time."

She only nodded to that.

He finished his sandwich and pushed his plate away, then leaned back. "Shall we get to some of the hard questions we've both been avoiding?"

She laughed and he just smiled. Damn he was smart and she loved that about him.

And that look in his eye told her that he loved when she laughed as well.

"So ask away," she said. "I promise I'll tell you the truth no matter what."

He nodded. "The boys seemed to be stunned at how far away your home world is. How long did it take you to get here?"

"I didn't come from my home world directly here," she said. "I was working on another planet in this area of this galaxy, so the trip didn't take that long. A week or so to get into position. But if I was on a fast ship directly from my home world to here, it would take about a half year."

He nodded to that and seemed to file it away.

"Explain to me how humans have spread so far in space? I remember a little of what you said on the ship, but my attention was elsewhere."

"Fair enough," she said, taking a sip of a soda and then sitting back so she could look at him directly.

"A very long time ago," she said, "from a planet so distant from here that no one I know of even knows where it might be, the first humans evolved and jumped into space."

"How long ago?" he asked.

She shrugged. "Some say only hundreds of thousands of years ago, others say millions and millions of years ago. I tend to go to the millions of years ago number."

He nodded. "Can't say I understand that kind of number, but go on."

"After the first humans spread out to the stars, they discovered that they were alone. There are no alien cultures out there that anyone knows about. None in this galaxy, my galaxy, or any galaxy close to here."

"So humans really are alone in the cosmos," he said.

"As far as anyone has found so far, yes," she said. Then she went on. "Those early humans figured out a way to seed humanity on planets that could support life. They also seeded all plant and animal life from the original first human home, so every planet with humans on it has the same plants and animals around them."

"Wow, that's a job," Benny said, shaking his head.

"It is," she said. "The Seeders, as we are called, are very good at this now after all this time."

"So you help with this seeding?" Benny asked.

"No," she said. "The front line of the seeding ships has already left this galaxy. They are working in the Andromeda galaxy. My job as a Seeder is to help the cultures start to mature. I get involved in one fashion or another in the growing cultures to help them get past certain disaster points and grow. I embed in cultures, as I am doing now, to help with what I can help with."

"How often have you done that?" he asked.

149

She took a deep breath. This was the first major problem point and from here on out she might lose this man. And that scared her to death.

"I promised I would tell you the complete truth, remember?" she said.

He nodded, looking very serious.

"This is my tenth time embedding in a culture on ten different planets."

A frown crossed his face. "So tell me what you are worried about in how that is possible for you to do that and still look as good as you do."

She smiled at that and nodded. "Thank you."

"Just truth," he said, smiling at her and her stomach twisted even harder. She was deathly afraid she was about to have Benny start hating her.

"I like this feeling between us," she said. "And I don't want to lose that, so I'm afraid of telling you a lot of this."

"Trust me to deal with what you are saying," he said.

She nodded.

"Seeders are picked to be sort of the guiding hands of cultures for thousands of years as they grow and develop and jump into space. We do not get sick, nor do we age, and we have memories that can remember just about anything. We can also do this."

She teleported to a place thirty steps from him and he damn near went over backwards.

She teleported back into her chair.

She had to show him that she wasn't a normal woman and that was one of the quickest ways she could think to do it.

"That's got to come in real handy," he said, his voice only cracking once as he adjusted his chair.

"So to answer your question truthfully and directly," she said. "I was born just over 200 years ago. And there is no upper limit on how long I can live barring accidents. I have heard of some Seeders being thousands of years old. Maybe older for all I know."

He sat there staring at her for the longest time while her heart almost beat out of her chest with worry. Then he said, "You look damn good for an old broad."

For a moment she didn't completely understand, then he smiled slightly and she laughed.

"Well, thank you," she said. "I guess."

He looked hard at her and then said, "Why do I get the sense you aren't telling me something really important."

She leaned forward and reached her hand across the table, offering it to Benny.

After a moment's hesitation, he took it.

She could feel the incredible attraction of the man pulling at her. His strong, work-worn hand rested in her hand and she kept her gaze locked on his dark, intense eyes.

"The reason you remember the ship," she said, "is because you have the Seeder gene as well. You could be a Seeder as well if you wanted."

He actually jerked at that, but didn't let go of her hand.

She squeezed his hand and then sat back, pulling away from touching him so he could just think.

"Besides living a long time," he said after a moment, "what does being a Seeder really mean?"

"It means that your life mission becomes to help all humans and humanity," she said, "no matter what planet they are on."

"And how many planets is that?" he asked.

"Do you have any idea how many people were in this city before the disaster?" she asked.

"Millions and millions," he said, "if you count all the boroughs across the rivers."

"There are more seeded human planets in just this galaxy than humans who used to be in this city."

"Oh," was all he said.

She let him sit in silence. At least he wasn't storming off. She wasn't sure what she would have been doing if the situations were reversed.

"And how many Seeders are there?" he asked.

"Not enough," she said. "Never enough, which is why I hope you'll join us."

"I'm not much of a joiner," he said.

"You don't join Seeders like joining some lodge," she said. "This is all a job and we all get paid for it."

"You get paid for helping people and living a long time?" he asked, looking directly at her.

"I do," she said, nodding. "And to be honest, I can't imagine a better job."

He nodded to that and sat back.

She just sat there, trying not to hold her breath in worry.

Finally he spoke again. "And after all this time you aren't married or have a boyfriend?"

"Never married," she said, "but I had some boyfriends

along the way, but never one that was a Seeder, so I always had to leave them after a decade or so."

"Because you didn't age," he said.

She nodded. "And my job moved me on. So no, I have no boyfriend now."

"And you are telling me the complete truth on everything?" he asked.

"I am," she said.

He looked at her. "So tell me the truth on this question. Are you attracted to me?"

She laughed and then stared him right in the eye. "More than I want to let myself believe. It's every damn thing I can do to not drag you into that bedroom."

"Oh, great," he said, smiling at her. "A woman with self-restraint."

CHAPTER 33

He had enjoyed the lunch and the conversation with Gina more than he wanted to admit. She was smart and attractive and funny.

And clearly she was attracted to him as much as he was to her.

But then when she started really telling him about herself, including how old she really was, he felt just stunned.

And when she just vanished from her chair and appeared across the room, then appeared back in her chair, he had damn near gone over backwards.

He wasn't sure what he had been expecting from a woman from space, but that had shocked him.

And her age, for a moment had shocked him as well.

But what had shocked him more than anything was her telling him that he had a special gene that allowed him to join her organization if he wanted. And that was why he had remembered her and the spaceship.

He really didn't understand everything she had told him. But he did understand when she said she could barely keep from taking him into the bedroom.

That he liked and understood completely, because he felt the same way about her.

After she said that he stood, indicating that she should remain where she was.

He moved over to the stairway door and bolted it closed as she watched.

Then he came back over to her and took her hand and helped her to her feet.

Then he kissed her.

For an instant she seemed shocked, then she melted against him, her perfect body pushing into his as her lips matched his.

He had kissed his share of women over the years, but that felt like a combination of a first kiss with a first girlfriend and kissing someone who he had kissed forever.

It was both perfect and exciting at the same time.

They fit together.

The kiss seemed to last for a very long time, then finally he pulled back and she looked at him. They were both almost the same height, so she looked him right in the eye, which he liked.

Her face was red and flushed and he had a hunch his was as well.

"Sorry," he said, smiling, "I just don't have as much self-restraint as you do."

She laughed, then said, "Well, you killed mine with that kiss, that's for sure."

With that, she took his hand and led the way into his bedroom. She kissed him again as they stood beside the bed. Then she pushed back and started unbuttoning her shirt.

He stood there, staring, more than likely his mouth open.

She pulled off her shirt and tossed it to one side, leaving her in jeans and a sports bra.

Wow.

She smiled at him. "You're falling behind."

Then she unzipped her jeans and slid them down over her hips, showing him her black panties.

She had to be the most attractive and in-shape woman he had ever seen or met.

He pulled his shirt over his head and tossed it to one side, then took off his pants as well as she slipped her sports bra over her head and then took off her underwear, exposing a small area of dark hair.

He took his pants off, showing her that he was about as aroused as a man could get.

She stared at him for a moment, then went into his arms, putting his penis between her legs and kissing him, pressing against him.

And he kissed back.

He pushed back into her strong arms, enjoying the feel of her breasts smashed into his chest, her legs holding his penis.

Finally, he pulled away, picked her up and put her on the bed.

She pulled him down on top of her and he was inside her.

Then he lost all track of time and emotions and everything as he made love to the woman of his dreams.

CHAPTER 34

Gina lay wrapped in Benny's strong arms, her head on his shoulder, her right leg over him.

She was still breathing hard and trembling from the number of orgasms she had had.

Benny's chest was raising and falling as he too worked to recover. His skin felt hot and wonderful to her.

Everything about this man felt right.

And making love to him had felt perfect, as if they belonged together.

One part of her mind wondered how that was even possible while another part didn't care. She just wanted to enjoy being with him more and more.

She pressed against him, not wanting to move.

"It seems," he said, "that when we're together, self-restraint might be a problem."

She laughed. "Trust me, what we just did will never be a problem for me."

"Me either," he said, turning his head to her and kissing her again, just long enough to make it clear he cared, but not long enough to get things started again.

"I got to ask another question," he said, staring up at the ceiling. "A serious one."

"Go ahead," she said.

"If I joined on to being a Seeder," he said, "would we leave here?"

"No," she said. "When I discovered you had the Seeder gene, I asked Chairman Carson if I could recruit you to help. I figure the two of us here could get a lot more done together than if I was trying to hide from you."

"Chairman Carson?" Benny asked.

"The man who gave the speech on the ship. Seeder ships, and most human spaceships from other planets, are all businesses. And everyone on board is hired to do a job. So instead of having captains, the person who runs a Seeder ship is called a chairman."

"As in chairman of the board?" Benny asked.

"Exactly," she said.

"So we would remain here, helping here, working together?" Benny asked.

"We would," she said.

"And how would you feel about that?" he asked.

She pushed her naked body into his and kissed his cheek.

"Besides the sex," he said, trying not to laugh.

She stopped and chuckled. "Honestly, I think we could be a fantastic team and help a lot more people together than we ever could apart. And I like the idea of working with you a great deal."

"Seriously?" he asked.

"Seriously," she said. "Right from the first moment I saw you, I had a hunch we would be a good team. And I hoped beyond hope that you learning about me and Seeders wouldn't mess all that up. It didn't, did it?"

He could hear the worry suddenly in her voice. And that relaxed him even more.

"I got a lot of things to figure out," he said, turning and kissing her. Then he said, "But wanting to work with you isn't one of those things."

"Good," she said, kissing him again, this time with more passion.

She could feel his penis starting to stir again under her leg and she liked the idea of that.

"Hold on," he said, pulling back from the kiss. "One more question. Is there an easy way for me to learn all about Seeders? Some sort of brain meld or something?"

She laughed. "We have high-speed education systems that can help you learn something quickly, if that's what you mean."

"Perfect," he said. "I want to do that so I really understand before I agree to anything."

"Very smart thinking," she said.

Then he kissed her again and pulled her over on top of him.

A moment later he was back inside of her and time ended and all the problems she faced flew away for her for the moment as all she wanted was to make love to this fantastic man.

And she did.

For longer than she ever thought possible.

CHAPTER 35

Just over an hour later, they had managed to get untangled and get dressed and head down the stairs for some dinner. Outside the windows, the sun was still pretty high in the evening sky and he could tell it was a hot day out there.

Thankfully, with the two generators running air-conditioning, the floor had stayed cool.

Benny felt stunned at how good it had felt to make love to Gina. Perfect in more ways than he could even imagine.

And her body was stunning. Her skin was smooth, her hair soft, her muscles hard and firm. He doubted she had an extra ounce of fat on her. He would have to ask her later what she did for exercise. He had brought up to his floor a treadmill and some free weights, and he figured on decent days, he could run around the observation balcony a few floors up.

If he had ever thought to imagine his perfect woman, he

wouldn't have done that good a job in his imagination to even come close to Gina in reality.

She only had a few problems. She was from space and she was two hundred years old. But he was fairly certain he could deal with both of those.

They walked down the stairs hand-in-hand, like two kids on a first date, which he guessed this actually was.

Then just outside the door to the floor where the professor and the three kids lived, he turned and kissed her again.

"What's that for?" she asked, smiling at him.

"Because it feels good," he said, grinning like a kid in high school at her.

She kissed him then.

"What was that for?" he asked when she pulled away.

"Because it feels good and a promise for more later."

"Now that I like," he said.

He turned and pulled the stairway door open.

The professor and David were working on dinner at the kitchen counter they had moved in from a nearby furniture store. Freddy and Candice were sitting at the big wooden conference table they used as a kitchen table.

Candice was dressed in a blue blouse and jeans and she had her blonde hair combed and pulled back. She smiled at him when they entered.

He couldn't believe how really thrilled it made him feel to see Candice sitting there like that.

"Wow," Benny said, smiling back at Candice. "Wonderful to see you feeling better."

"Exhausted still," Candice said, "but I needed to get up and move around again."

Benny indicated Gina and introduced her.

"Thank you," Candice said, smiling at Gina. "The professor tells me you were carrying me here. I don't remember at all, other than thinking a beautiful angel had come to rescue me."

Benny agreed with both the beautiful and the angel part.

"You are more than welcome," Gina said. "And trust me, I'm really glad we met. You were the one that directed me here to this wonderful place and these great people. So I need to thank you for saving me."

Benny smiled at that fib. It was a perfect one. Gina really had a great way with making people feel right about themselves.

"I did?" Candice asked, looking surprised.

"When I met you on the street," Gina said, "you mumbled something about needing to get to the Empire State Building and then collapsed. So I brought you here."

Candice shook her head. "I don't remember any of that. But thank you for getting me here and getting me cleaned up."

"You would have done the same for me," Gina said, sitting down at the table across from Candice.

Benny took the seat across from Gina and nodded.

Candice was smiling, clearly feeling better. Benny figured that with one small lie, Gina just might have saved a life.

"So you like the apartment we set up?" Freddy asked.

"I do," Gina said, her voice enthusiastic. "It's wonderful. Thank you all for allowing me to stay here. I promise I'll carry my weight."

"Before you two came in," Candice said, "we were talking about how Benny thinks there will be more people joining us. Do you think so as well?"

"I do," Gina said. "That's part of what Benny and I were talking about upstairs."

Benny nodded, really, really appreciating how smooth Gina was. "She has information about where some other groups are located, and where some single people are holed up."

"Some will see our lights," the professor said. "Others, I think we need to go talk to."

"I agree," Benny said. Then he looked at Gina. "Can you tell us which ones you met that might be good candidates for this building and if they would want to come here?"

"I met some of them," she said, nodding, "and saw a lot of lights at night after the power went out. I think I can find them again."

"This building is clearly large enough for more people," the professor said.

Benny couldn't agree more. And from what he remembered of some of those people while they were all in the spaceship, they needed a better place to stay and some of them would need help and a direction and a feeling there might be a future to just survive.

Gina changed the subject by asking Freddy what he had been studying in school.

Benny watched her be sociable, smiling easily, keeping the mood light and the questions away from the tragedy.

He flat wanted to spend a lot of time with her. As much as possible, actually. He knew that without a doubt.

Tonight, after dinner, Benny would ask Gina what benefits there would be for him being a Seeder as well in the coming years. If being able to jump around from place to place like she did was one of the things he would learn to do, that would be enough.

And a chance to be with her for a long time would be even more worth it.

CHAPTER 36

Gina enjoyed her dinner with the professor, his three charges, and Benny. The conversation was light and about survival. She knew that all of them had a lot of trauma to get through, but with time they would work through it.

And Gina had decided about halfway through dinner that she would help Candice. The girl had a real brain and if she could get past the next few weeks, she would be a real asset to the future of this planet.

After dinner, all of them showed Gina the other floors they had set up for more survivors. Each floor had once been offices, but now were set up to handle five or six people living comfortably in lots of room. Each floor had a number of bathrooms, had private bedrooms for everyone, and a community living area with kitchen and couches and big screens for movies.

They had done the work on eight different floors. Gina was flat impressed.

Then they went down a few more floors to offices that had not been set up.

"We have room here and in the three floors below this one for more people. Each floor would hold six or seven more people."

"I honestly don't want to go back out into that smell right now," Candice said.

Gina moved over and put her arm around the young girl. "I have a hunch we can wait until things calm into the fall before worrying about these rooms."

"I agree," Benny said. "Candice, I don't see you needing to go back out there anytime soon, to be honest with you."

"Thank you," she said softly.

Gina kept her arm around the young girl and together they went to an elevator.

"Working on a generator?" Gina asked.

"Starts up when the button is pushed," Benny said. "And only this one elevator works. As we go up I'll tell you how to get out of one if it stops or gets stuck."

"Thank you," Gina said, suddenly realizing she hadn't even given that any thought since she could teleport anywhere if she needed to.

When they got back to the main floor, Gina asked Candice how she was doing.

"Tired," Candice said.

Gina led the young girl into her bedroom and closed the door behind her.

Candice dropped on the bed. "I'm so glad I'm back here."

"I think everyone is glad you are as well," Gina said, smiling, "in case you can't tell."

"I can," she said, her voice quivering a little. "They are my new family, aren't they?"

"They are," Gina said. "And you couldn't ask for a better group. We all are family now, and we all have to work together."

Candice nodded, clearly getting more tired by the moment.

"Crawl in and get some sleep," Gina said. You are safe here. And if you need something, I'll be here. Us girls got to stick together, you know."

Candice smiled at that and nodded. "Thank you for carrying me here."

"Thank you for getting me to this wonderful group of people," Gina said.

Then she stood and headed for the door. "Sleep well."

"I think tonight I will," Candice said.

Gina went back out into the main area and pulled the door closed behind her.

Benny was cooking something in the kitchen and he glanced up at her and she nodded.

She could hear the professor and the two boys talking in the living room area about movies. Benny was working on making them some popcorn.

"She going to be all right?" Benny asked, indicating Candice's room.

"I think she might be now," Gina said, moving over and leaning against a counter so she could see Benny.

"Great work with her," Benny said.

Gina nodded. "She's going to have some rough patches, as everyone will. The key is for us to help them through the bad times as much as possible."

Benny glanced over at the living room area to make sure he couldn't be heard, then turned back to her. "Knowing there is a larger world out there and that we are getting support helps me more than I can tell you."

She nodded. "Too bad we can't tell everyone, but most would not believe it and many it would hurt instead of help."

"Found that out the hard way, huh?"

"On a lot of different worlds in a lot of different ways," she said. "It was why I had to have permission to even talk with you, even though you remembered the ship."

"Makes sense," he said as the wonderful-smelling popcorn started to pop.

"Are we joining them for a movie?" she asked.

He smiled at her. "I was kind of hoping you could give me a quick lesson on the Seeders."

She felt a huge feeling of relief wash over her. "That I would be glad to do."

"Then if we feel up for it, we can watch a movie and have popcorn upstairs."

"Perfect," she said. "Just perfect."

FORMING A TEAM

CHAPTER 37

After they delivered the popcorn to the guys in the living room, Benny both said goodnight to them and Gina thanked them again for allowing her in their building. Then they headed for the staircase. The sun was just setting to the west, the sky a beautiful orange with the sunset.

A few lights were shining through the dark city, but very few. Benny felt they needed to get out there, start trying to help people, but he was going to need to depend on Gina to guide them in the best way of doing that.

And who to even approach without getting shot on sight.

"You ready to get some information," Gina asked as they closed the door to the apartment and stopped on the landing outside the door.

"We need to lock up this staircase door at our floor," Benny said, suddenly realizing what she was intending. "Just in case someone comes up to find us for some reason or another."

"Good thinking," she said.

An instant later they were inside the door on their floor.

It took him a second to get his bearings, but not long.

"Wow," Benny said. "I could get used to doing that."

"Can't ever let anyone see you do it, though," she said.

He showed her how to lock up, then turned to her.

His stomach was doing flip-flops and he had a hunch he was sweating slightly.

"You trust me?" she asked.

"I do," he said. "But keep in mind all this space stuff is not anything I ever once thought about before meeting you."

She stepped up and kissed him hard. Then she stepped back and looked at him.

He honestly had to admit her kiss calmed him some, in some ways, and excited him in others.

"I honestly do remember what that feels like," she said. "I was twenty-eight, working with relief groups on a major flooding disaster on my planet. My planet had been in space for a hundred years or so, but I sure never thought of going. My job was in the mud helping people survive and rebuild."

"Recruited?" Benny asked.

She nodded. "One of the women working beside me asked me if I would be interested in helping out on a much larger scale. I said sure. But let me tell you, I didn't handle learning about Seeders anyway near as well as you are."

"Oh, I'm screaming and running in my mind," Benny said. "Just never learned how to do that in real life."

"Lucky for me," she said, kissing him again.

She turned to the air. "Captain Carson, Benny Slade and I would like to talk with you for a moment."

She nodded. "Thank you, chairman."

Then Benny watched as she said into thin air, "Two transporting aboard."

She nodded a moment later and turned to Benny. "Here we go."

The next moment they were standing in the same position in a large office.

The place had a few soft chairs, a tan couch, and a huge wooden desk. The carpet under Benny's feet was soft and the air smelled fresh.

Pictures of children hung on one wall, while the other white walls were decorated in photos of beautiful scenes of waterfalls and sand dunes.

The man who had spoken to everyone in the big room was coming around the desk, his hand out, smiling.

Benny shook his hand.

"Chairman Carson, this is Benny Slade," Gina said.

"Great meeting you," the chairman said, shaking Benny's hand with a firm handshake.

The man had dark eyes and the smile on his face was also in his eyes.

"Great meeting you as well, sir," Benny said.

"No sir on these ships," the chairman said. "Just chairman is fine."

Benny nodded, looking around at the large and comfortable office. "I'm back on the ship I presume?"

"You are," the chairman said. "Are you interested in joining us, I hope?"

"Benny wants to know more about Seeders history and what we do and why," Gina said. "Before he makes up his mind."

Benny nodded to that.

"Sensible," the chairman said. "But I do hope you decide to join us. We can use all the help we can get in the mess below."

"I'm going to help with that," Benny said, "even if I don't join your people."

"Of that I have no doubt," the chairman said. "But we need help in the long-term planning to get the survivors back into full civilization as soon as possible, and that's what we really need the help with."

"You're thinking years down the road already?" Benny asked, kind of stunned.

"Decades and centuries," the chairman said.

Benny didn't even know what to think about that.

Then the chairman turned to Gina. "You thinking basic overall lesson?"

"I am," Gina said. "Won't take more than an hour, but will give Benny all the information he needs to decide without me trying to explain it all."

"You have my permission," he said.

He reached out and shook Benny's hand again. "I hope we can talk soon."

"Thank you, Chairman," Gina said.

"Yes, thank you," Benny said.

A moment later they were standing in a very comfortable

apartment. A thin blanket lay scattered on a couch, paperwork covered a coffee table along with some dirty dishes.

He could see a dining table and a kitchen beyond.

Everything was in brown tones and photos of beautiful natural scenes were scattered along the walls, some of which looked slightly alien in nature.

"This is my apartment," Gina said.

"On the ship?" Benny asked.

"On the ship," Gina nodded. "Sorry for the mess. It was a rough few days getting ready to join you."

Benny actually liked that the apartment looked lived in. If it had been spotless, he would have worried.

She led the way into a side office with three large screens and a comfortable chair.

She tapped a spot on the desktop and the screens came alive. She dropped into the chair like she had done so for a very long time, her fingers moving over a panel he could barely see in front of her.

The image of the main area in the Empire State Building came up. The boys and the professor were still watching television.

Gina's hands moved and she quickly checked in on Candice. She was sound asleep.

Then Gina pulled the image back out so it felt like a plane over New York. The city was dotted with green lights.

Gina shook her head, then sadly she said. "We lost three more today."

"How many are there on the island now?" Benny asked, kneeling down beside her so he could see her screen clearly.

The four green dots in the Empire State Building were clear. And in another high rise building about twenty blocks to the north there were another seven green dots.

The rest were scattered, mostly solo.

Benny didn't want to think about being alone in all that smell. Survival, or any reason for survival, would seem like a distant thought. They had to help some of these people.

Gina quickly cleared the board and brought up another screen. Then in a drawer to her right she dug out two ear buds.

She stood and gestured for him to sit in the chair.

He did, feeling odd being in her chair.

She handed him the two ear buds. "Put those in your ears and face the main screen."

"What will happen?" he asked.

"Over about an hour you will be given all the history we know of the Seeders, what we can all do as far as skills, what you would need to do to join, and our mission statement. All that basic stuff."

"So I just sit and watch?"

She nodded. "It will feed you the information as fast as you can absorb it. It mostly takes about an hour. At least that's what it took for me. You won't feel the time going by."

"What will you be doing?" he asked.

"Cleaning my apartment," she said, smiling. "And doing some dishes."

"Can't say I'm not scared about this," he said.

"Just think of it as a movie without popcorn."

He took a deep breath, moving his shoulders and neck around, then exhaled. She remembered how scared she had been with this first introduction. But after that, she hadn't been afraid at all.

"I'm ready," he said, putting the two ear buds in.

"See you shortly," she said.

Then she pressed the start button.

CHAPTER 38

Gina pushed the button and saw the images start to flash past in front of Benny. He didn't stiffen or anything, just sat there, staring straight ahead.

He was incredibly handsome. She could just stare at him, and she had a hard time believing he was really sitting here in her office, in her apartment, on the ship.

She sure hoped he decided to join the Seeders.

She was starting to wonder what this future job would be like without him working with her.

She turned and headed for the door. Her apartment needed a good cleaning and the dishes would start smelling if she didn't do something with them soon. This hour was as good a time as any to do that.

She was almost out the door when behind her Benny said, "Wow, that was something."

She spun around and went back to her screens as he pushed back and pulled the ear buds out.

She quickly checked the program. It had run completely.

He had absorbed that entire program in less than three minutes.

How was that possible?

"You all right?" she asked as he put the buds on the desktop.

"I'm fine, and impressed," he said. "Can't imagine why a group like the Seeders would want a city boy from a backwards planet to join up. But it sure has some nice perks, from what I can tell."

She opened her mouth, than shut it, then opened it again, then shut it again.

He looked at her. "Is there something wrong?"

"I honestly don't know," she said, her stomach twisting and fear clamping down on her stomach.

"Chairman Carson, permission to talk with you?" she said into the air.

"Granted," he said.

"Something's wrong, isn't it?" Benny asked, worry filling his eyes.

"We'll find out in a minute," she said, and transported them to the chairman's office.

He seemed to be surprised that Benny was with her. When they both appeared, he frowned.

"Change your mind?" the chairman asked.

"Actually, no," Benny said, smiling. "I'm pretty convinced I like what I saw."

The chairman glanced at Gina and she nodded.

"Three minutes," she said.

"Holy shit," the chairman said.

Then the chairman looked up slightly. "Chairman Ray, would it be possible for you to join me?"

A moment later Gina was stunned again as one of the most powerful and oldest of all Seeders appeared in the room. He glanced at Chairman Carson, then strode over and extended his hand. "My name is Chairman Wade Ray."

"Benny Slade," Benny said. "Nice to meet you."

Chairman Ray looked at Benny and stepped back. "Have you decided to join us?"

"Just took the introduction video," Benny said. "I want to sleep on it, but I like what I've seen so far."

"He did the introduction video in three minutes," Gina said.

Benny looked at her. "I thought you said it was going to take me an hour."

"It took me an hour," she said, smiling at him, but she couldn't make her stomach stop worrying about what this might mean.

"It takes most people an hour," Chairman Ray said, smiling. "But not all. Just as your memory could not be wiped clear of your time on the ship, the Seeder gene you carry is so strong, it allowed you to absorb that lesson almost instantly."

"And what exactly does that mean?" Benny asked, clearly as worried as Gina felt.

"It means I hope very much you decide to join us," Chairman Ray said, smiling.

"And if I did, would I be able to stay here and help my planet recover?" Benny asked.

"We would desperately need you to do just that," Chairman Ray said. "And help us all plan the future recovery."

Benny nodded and Gina let out a sigh of relief. There was real hope that Benny would join the Seeders.

"Do me a favor, would you?" Chairman Ray asked Benny. "You saw in the training how Seeders can jump from one spot to another? And I assume Ms. Helm has shown you as well."

Benny nodded.

Chairman Ray stepped back closer to the wall. "Imagine yourself standing here beside me looking at Ms. Helm."

"I'm not sure what you mean?" Benny asked.

"Just believe you are standing beside me, facing Gina Helm. Close your eyes and try it for me once. Just believe you are here."

Gina watched as Benny shrugged. She had no idea what Chairman Ray was trying to do.

Benny closed his eyes and a moment later he was standing beside Chairman Ray.

Gina covered her mouth to not allow the gasp to come out.

Benny opened his eyes and staggered back against the wall in shock, shaking one of Chairman Carson's pictures, but not knocking it down.

"Did you do that?" Benny asked.

Chairman Ray just shook his head and smiled. "You are a natural Seeder, the gene is so strong in you. There are four others like you on this planet. We made sure all four survived and none of them remember the rescue because we had spotted them ahead of time and kept them knocked out. We didn't find you until the transport."

Gina opened her mouth and then shut it. She had no idea what to say or even what it meant for a Seeder to have a strong gene. She didn't even know Seeders had special genes until earlier today.

"Is this normal to have five naturals on one developing planet?" Chairman Carson asked.

"So far, this is the only five we have found in this galaxy," Chairman Ray said.

Then he looked at Gina. "No one told you, but you were a natural as well, only one of two in your galaxy so far. We hid that information from you because at that point we didn't know what to do."

Gina could feel her mouth opening, then closing.

She wanted to breathe, but doubted she could at the moment. She had no idea what it meant to be a natural, but she was stunned that Chairman Ray and others had known about her and followed her.

Chairman Ray smiled. "I would say you two have a lot to talk about. I hope you will take our formal training, Benny Slade. I have a hunch it won't take long."

"What would happen if I decided to do so," Benny asked.

Chairman Ray smiled. "Then I would personally help both you and Gina develop to your full potential so you could help us save this planet."

Gina could say nothing. Her mind was gone.

Chairman Ray knew about her when she was recruited. She

kept thinking about that over and over. She didn't feel special, at least no more than any other Seeder.

Chairman Ray nodded to them, then to Chairman Carson.

And then he vanished.

Gina just wanted her mind to return. One solid thought.

Anything.

"How far away is he going right now?" Benny asked, staring at the spot where Chairman Ray had been.

"No telling," Chairman Carson said. "Across the galaxy, maybe. A couple hundred thousand light years, maybe. No way of knowing."

Benny laughed. "At some point I really need to learn how far both of those measurements are."

CHAPTER 39

Benny had no idea what had happened, exactly, in the chairman's office, or even who this Chairman Wade Ray was. The guy seemed important, but Benny would have to ask Gina later about that.

But right now Gina seemed as stunned as he was feeling.

The training information was now in his mind and he could remember it all when he focused on it.

He knew Seeders were humans that went from galaxy to galaxy seeding the human race on Earth-like planets. And then hundreds of thousands of Seeders remained behind the front line to help out the planted humans advance and get past all the self-destruction points to become advanced democratic cultures.

Many Seeders just remained and settled on the planets they helped, others, like Gina, moved around.

There was no information about any sort of "natural seeder" people in the introduction program. Not a word.

However, it had talked some about the ability of Seeders to transport, but it said in the video that took training. Seemed he could do that already. It scared him to think about that. Training sounded like a damned good idea when it came to jumping all over the place.

Gina, after a moment, seemed to recover slightly and nodded to Chairman Carson. "We'll talk with you soon, I'm sure."

The chairman nodded and Gina jumped them to her apartment.

Again he was impressed on how comfortable her apartment felt, but he really wanted to be back in the city.

"How about we go to our apartments on the surface?" Benny said. "I think I need to be a little grounded."

Gina nodded. "Two to transport to the surface," she said in the general direction of the ceiling. At some point he'd ask her why she did that.

A moment later they were standing in Benny's living room.

Around them, out the windows, the once bright city was dark, only shadows of buildings like ghosts in the summer night. Overhead the stars were bright, filling the summer sky. More than likely this was one of the first times the stars could be seen from downtown Manhattan in a hundred years.

He knew those stars out there were full of humans. The idea of that just stunned him.

And after he helped this planet recover, he could go out there if he wanted to.

The idea of that flat scared him more than he wanted to admit.

He moved over to the kitchen area and pulled out a popcorn maker and started it up.

Gina had not said a word since they got back. She had gone around and sat down on the couch staring out into the dark night and all the stars beyond the windows.

He poured them both a glass of white wine, even though he wasn't sure if she even liked wine, and walked over and set both glasses down on the coffee table in front of her.

Then, saying nothing, he went back to the kitchen area to wait for the popcorn to pop. He was pretty sure she hadn't even noticed him.

Finally, when he had a large bowl done and two glasses of ice water as well, he went back to the couch and sat down a little distance from her.

He put the green plastic bowl of popcorn between them. It smelled wonderful and he had salted it, again without asking if she liked popcorn or salt on popcorn.

He set her glass of water beside her untouched glass of wine, then leaned back sort of sideways on the couch so he could see her beautiful face. Her gaze was distant, not really in the room. He had no idea what she was thinking about, but he needed to find out.

And he needed some answers as well.

"Mind telling me who this Chairman Ray person is?"

She seemed to come back into her eyes at that point, then nodded.

She took a drink of water, then seemed to see the wine for

the first time when she set her water glass down. She picked up the wine and sipped it.

"This is good," she said. "Thanks."

He took a drink of wine as well, then a handful of popcorn, waiting for her to answer his question.

"As far as I know," she said, holding the wine in her hands, "Chairman Ray is one of the oldest and most powerful of all Seeders. No one knows how old he really is, but he and his wife are rumored to be maybe two hundred thousand years old, if not more."

Benny had the popcorn half-chewed when she said that. His mind told him from the information he had gotten in the training program that extreme long age was possible. But grasping that kind of age was far, far beyond him.

He was still having issues with the fact that Gina was two hundred years old.

"Powerful how?" Benny asked, pushing the age part back. "My understanding from the training thing is that there is no real organization that runs the Seeders."

"That's true," Gina said, "as far as I know. But with age comes respect and the oldest tend to help plan things. But realize, I haven't had much more Seeder history than what you got earlier."

"So I have some special Seeder gene, more so than most Seeders, and it seems so do you," Benny said. "Any idea exactly what that means?"

"Not a clue," she said. "I wish I did. I didn't even know there was such a thing as a Seeder gene until they told me that was the reason you could remember the ship."

Benny realized that in the training program he had gone through, there was not one word about that either.

"So we're both kind of flying in the dark here," he said.

"Pitch dark," she said.

She took another sip of wine and nodded. "You would think after two hundred years, this kind of thing wouldn't happen to me. I feel like I did when I was approached to be a Seeder. Confused and puzzled."

"Good," he said. "That makes two of us."

She laughed and set her wine down and took a handful of popcorn. After she tasted a handful she smiled. "Perfect."

"So do you think I should join?" he asked. "Get the training?"

"That's up to you," she said.

"Have you ever regretted it?"

"Not for an instant," she said.

"So I know it's my decision," Benny said. "But I could use your opinion."

"My personal opinion is that I want you to join for selfish reasons," she said. "I want to work with you, get to know you better, and save a lot of people with you."

"Some of that doesn't sound so selfish," he said. "But we can do that without me joining."

"For a while," she said, nodding. "But I have a hunch if you could do some of the things I can do, and we both get whatever advanced training Chairman Ray is talking about, we will be even more effective. And save even more people."

Benny glanced out over the dark city. He remembered clearly those green lights on the screen in Gina's apartment on the ship. Each person, each green light, needed help. And some needed it quickly or they would not survive for long.

He had to make this decision quickly. And then get on with the job at hand.

"Let me sleep on this for the night," he said. "And I'll have a decision in the morning."

"Good idea," she said, nodding.

"But honestly," he said, "I'm leaning toward signing up."

When he said that, it felt right.

She smiled. "I hope you keep leaning."

"So one more question and then we can relax and watch a movie or something," he said.

"Anything," she said.

"How far is a light year?"

She looked at him for a moment, then laughed. "Light travels at one-hundred-and-eighty-six thousand miles per second."

He nodded. He remembered that from school somewhere.

"A light year is how far light travels in one year's time," she said.

And once again he couldn't imagine that distance. He got the thousands part.

He shook his head. "Some way to relay to me how big this galaxy is?" he said.

"There are billions of stars in this galaxy. Many billions."

He nodded, looking out at the stars.

"If this planet was represented by one speck of dust here on the coffee table," she said. "Using that scale of this planet as a speck of dust, this galaxy would be far, far, far bigger than this planet."

"And there are a lot of galaxies?" he asked, trying to even pretend to grasp that much distance.

"Billions," she said.

And once again he couldn't imagine the size and scale. "I think I'm going to need one of your learning programs to actually understand any of this. Sorry I asked."

She laughed, moved the popcorn bowl to the table and came over and leaned against him, putting her head against his chest and stretching out on the couch.

Damn that felt good.

And it felt right.

And tomorrow when he woke up he knew what decision he was going to make.

He was joining this beautiful woman. In every way he could.

CHAPTER 40

Gina awoke the next morning to the smell of bacon and toast cooking.

The sun was just coming up over the city and the sky was a deep blue. The water around the island looked calm and a dark gray, contrasting with the metal and steel and stone of the giant structures around them.

This city was a beautiful place, of that there was no doubt. She could see why Benny loved it so much.

Last night she and Benny had tried to watch a movie, but both of them had fallen asleep.

Benny woke her up after a short time and got her headed to her own bed in her apartment. She had made some groggy mention that she would like to sleep with him and he had said they both needed the sleep. And if she slept with him, neither of them would sleep.

She had known he was right.

And now, after sleeping, she did feel rested.

A moment later there was a knock on her door.

"Come in," she said, sitting up in bed and working to straighten out her bed hair. She had slept in a t-shirt and a pair of running shorts.

"Breakfast in ten minutes," he said, smiling at her.

Her heart damn near beat out of her chest. He was more attractive than before, if that was possible, standing there in his jeans, dress shirt with the sleeves rolled up, and a yellow plastic spatula in one hand.

"Smells wonderful," she said.

"Do you drink coffee?" he asked.

"I do," she said. "Black. Do I have time for a quick shower?"

"Make it real quick if you want warm eggs and toast," he said, smiling.

Then he turned away and headed back to the kitchen.

Eleven minutes later, showered and wearing jeans and a thin blue blouse with a sports bra under it, she padded into his kitchen with her shoes and socks in hand.

He was just serving up two eggs, light toast, and a slice of ham for each plate. He also had what looked to be orange juice in glasses at the table.

"I told the professor we were going to have breakfast up here," he said as she took her seat and he slid the plate in front of her.

The food smelled heavenly and she dug into the slice of ham, letting the slightly salty taste melt in her mouth.

He sat across from her, eating as well, and they didn't speak for a few minutes until finally he said, "I've decided to join up.

I can see no reason not to and about a thousand reasons to join."

She smiled, then stood and went around the table and kissed him, long and hard.

Just about the point where neither of them were going to finish their breakfasts, she pulled away and went back to her side of the table. She barely made it back. She really just wanted to make love to him right there.

He was smiling and she could feel that she was as well.

"How long will this training take?" he asked.

"Not a clue," she said. She pointed out over the city. "We don't have a lot of time for some of the people out there."

"I was thinking that," he said. "So after breakfast let's ask and then get to work."

"We'll do it from my office in the ship first," she said, "find the person who needs the most help soonest and get there."

"I was going to suggest the same thing," he said.

He finished his breakfast and pushed the plate away, taking one last sip of orange juice.

She did the same and they stood together.

"Door is still locked," he said, "and the professor won't be expecting us down there for a good hour or two."

She nodded. "Let's go find out what this training is all about."

She reached out and took his hand and he held it, his grasp firm in her hand, his skin wonderful against hers.

"Chairman Carson, would you contact Chairman Ray? Benny and I are ready to go."

"Wonderful," Chairman Carson said after a moment. "My office."

"You ready?" she asked Benny."

"Scared to death and I have a ton of doubts," he said. "Sort of like climbing on the old roller coaster on Coney Island back in the day. So why not?"

She nodded and squeezed his hand, not really knowing what he meant.

"I'm worried as well, but not scared of what's coming. I know it can only be good if we do it together."

"Now that I agree with," he said.

She again squeezed his hand and said, "Two to transport aboard."

Then a moment later she had them standing in Chairman Carson's office facing a smiling Chairman Wade Ray.

CHAPTER 41

enny smiled at the man with the long, gray hair and the broad smile.

"I'm ready to go, Chairman," Benny said. He indicated Gina. "We both are. Together."

Ray nodded. "That is fantastic to hear."

"How long is this training going to take?" Gina asked. "We have a lot of hurting people in that city below we need to get to and rescue."

Ray smiled, but his eyes were serious and Benny could tell that saving people was important to Ray. "Twenty minutes for the training, maybe another hour for me to answer your basic questions."

Benny nodded. They could take that time. It would be more than worth it, he had a hunch.

"We can do that," Gina said.

"We'll need to go to my ship in this galaxy first and pick up my wife Tacita," Ray said. "Then we will jump to another ship for the training."

Benny had no idea exactly what Ray meant, but he had a hunch he would in an hour or so.

Gina nodded. "Let's get started."

Chairman Ray glanced at the silent Chairman Carson. "We will return in an hour or so."

Carson only nodded.

A moment later Benny found himself standing on what looked like a conference room in a building. It had no windows and only a long table surrounded by leather chairs that were pushed in. There were photos on the wall of various stars and beautiful images of colored clouds in space.

A woman with long black hair appeared next to Ray.

Ray said, "My wife, Chairman Tacita."

"An honor to meet you," Gina said, bowing slightly.

"Yes, an honor," Benny said, nodding toward the woman with the dark eyes and a slight smile.

Ray took Tacita's hand and a moment later they were standing on a massive control area of a ship. A good dozen people manned stations around the room the size of a small gym. And two white chairs molded together and facing front were down two levels.

Benny couldn't hear a thing. Everyone worked in silence at their stations, not even noticing that four people had arrived.

"Where are we?" Gina asked.

"This is the control bridge of our main ship," Ray said. "We are, at the moment, about seventy galaxies away from the Milky Way Galaxy."

Gina staggered a little and Benny put out his arm to hold her. She clearly understood distances. Maybe it was better, for the moment, that he didn't really understand just how far they had jumped in that instant of time.

"I've never seen a ship this size," Gina said after a moment.

"There are none this size in the Milky Way," Tacita said, her voice flat and matter-of-fact, "and won't be for another three hundred years."

"But two are on their way there now," Ray said.

Benny had no idea what any of this meant, but he had to admit that if this was just the control room of a ship, how huge was the ship itself? He didn't figure they would have time for a tour, since all this was only supposed to take just over an hour.

Ray led them over to two chairs against a far wall facing two large screens and indicated that they should sit.

Gina did and Benny found himself only hesitating for a moment before sitting down as well.

The chair looked like a hard plastic, but it molded around him and supported his back perfectly as he sat down. Nice invention.

"Please put both hands on the surface in front of you," Ray said.

Benny did at the same time Gina did beside him.

And that was the last thing he remembered about being in that large bridge until Chairman Ray said that they could sit back.

He felt like he had just had every bit of information in the New York City Library forced into his brain, organized, and stored.

203

And so, so much more.

He knew that now he was a Seeder. In all respects.

He stood and Gina slowly stood beside him, her hand on his arm for support.

Then Benny looked up into the eyes of Chairman Ray and Chairman Tacita and bowed slightly. He knew them, he knew that they were much, much older than even rumored, that this ship they were on was the first Seeder Mother Ship, and so much more.

"Thank you for this honor," Benny said. And he meant it. More than he had ever meant anything in his life.

"Yes, thank you," Gina said, and she also bowed slightly.

A moment later the four of them were in a very comfortable lounge with four chairs and light crackers and cheeses and glasses of water on a wooden coffee table in the center. Each chair was an overstuffed brown leather chair and as Benny sat, again the chair formed comfortably around him.

After all four of them were seated, Chairman Ray said, "That process took exactly twenty-one minutes. You have been gone now from Chairman Carson's ship for just under thirty minutes. I know time is of the essence to you at this point in the rescue, but I hope you will take this next hour to ask us any question you feel is necessary."

Benny looked over at Gina and she nodded.

"We can take the time," he said.

Benny now understood exactly how far they were from his New York City and the Milky Way Galaxy. He just understood it. He wasn't sure how, but he understood it now and was impressed. But he had one question he still didn't understand.

"All Seeders have a Seeder gene," Benny said. "What makes the one we have so special? Does it give us extra powers?"

Ray smiled. "Not so much, but in a way, yes. You can remember things over centuries better than others and you both have the ability to transport vast distances, far greater distances than any normal Seeder."

"But the biggest factor is that the gene," Tacita said, "gives you the ability to chairman with a partner one of these mother ships."

"Oh," Benny said, sitting back. In his mind the size of a Seeder mother ship was clear. They were as large as most moons. And could carry millions of people.

"Wow," Gina said.

They talked for another thirty minutes, Benny just confirming basic knowledge he had in his mind more than anything else.

Finally he said something that had been bothering him, because he knew that Seeders, especially Seeders like Ray and Tacita, never did much of anything without a plan.

"So with me and Gina now working on my home world, that makes six of us there, four you saved from the disaster twice."

"Actually," Ray said, "Since yesterday we found yet another who survived. And another showed up just after the last wave hit from another local planet. They have teamed up and both are being recruited."

"So eight there," Benny said. "What is it, the water?"

"We honestly don't know," Tacita said.

"So what is your plan for all of us?"

"We want you all to help save the population of your planet first and foremost," Ray said, "along with thousands of other Seeders helping out around your planet."

"But after that is stable?" Benny asked, leaning forward.

Ray smiled. "We hope you and Gina in a few years will recruit the other four."

"We can do that," Benny said. "And then what?"

"If we could see into the future," Tacita said, "we would."

"But we can't," Ray said smiling.

Benny nodded. He knew that, for the moment, Ray and Tacita didn't want to talk about any possible plans. And that honestly made sense to Benny. He and Gina needed to concentrate on saving lives.

And finding a new way for people on his Earth to live going forward.

Benny stood and Gina did as well, slightly ahead of Ray and Tacita.

"It's time we get started," Benny said.

"I agree," Ray said.

Ray reached over and took Tacita's hand and an instant later they were back in Chairman Carson's office.

Carson jumped to his feet and bowed slightly to all of them.

"I'm glad you have joined us," Ray said to Benny. "Good luck in this coming battle."

"Yes," Tacita said. "Best success."

And with that they were both gone.

Benny glanced at the startled face of Chairman Carson. "Thank you, Chairman, for the use of your office."

"Yes, thank you," Gina said.

"Any time," Carson said.

"Shall we go to work?" Benny asked Gina.

"Let's do it," she said, giving him that smile he was coming to love more than anything.

A moment later, side-by-side, they were bent over a screen in her apartment office, their shoulders touching as they studied the green dots and the notes Gina had made about each person.

Even though Benny now understood the vast expanse of human worlds out there in the stars, even though this was his first day as a Seeder, his only focus was on his home city, his home planet, and saving as many people as he could as quickly as he could.

There would be time later to really think about what had happened. And what he had agreed to.

The larger Seeders Universe would take time for him to understand. But many people out there in his home city amid all the death didn't have time.

So he was focused.

And he knew that the woman of his dreams beside him felt exactly the same way.

They needed to quickly find survivors.

And then together rescue them.

After all, saving human life, human cultures, was what Seeders did.

He was now a Seeder. And that felt exactly right.

USA TODAY BESTSELLING AUTHOR

DEAN WESLEY
SMITH

STAR MIST

A SEEDERS UNIVERSE NOVEL

If you enjoyed *The High Edge*, try the next thrilling novel in the
Seeders Universe series, *Star Mist*! What follows is a sample
chapter.

PROLOGUE

The alien ship looked more like a large pile of black and gray garbage smashed together into a large ball than a spaceship hanging there in the blackness of space just beyond the edge of the Milky Way Galaxy.

Yet Chairman Wade Ray knew it was a ship.

And that ship was the most important discovery in hundreds and hundreds of thousands of years of human history.

Chairman Wade Ray stood, his hands behind his back, in the command center of his ship, staring at the image of the alien ship on the huge monitor that filled one wall of the command center. Ray had his long, silver-gray hair pulled back as always and wore a dark-silk dress shirt and dark slacks and soft leather shoes.

He could feel the tension around him in the huge room like a heavy blanket on a warm night.

Sixteen people manned stations behind him and not a one could be heard. They all felt as he felt, that what they were seeing couldn't be possible.

Tacita, his wife and partner and co-chairman of this ship, stood beside him, also just studying the strange shape of the alien ship. She had her hair extremely short and wore a black silk pantsuit.

To Ray, she was the most beautiful woman he had ever seen and he had been in love with her for more years than he wanted to think about.

He couldn't imagine ever not having her brilliant mind and sharp wit working beside him.

Especially now, when they faced an alien ship.

He shook his head. How was this even possible?

No alien race in thousands and thousands of galaxies had ever managed to survive long enough to build even a galaxy-wide civilization, let alone a ship that could travel the vast distances between galaxies. When the Seeder scout ships discover an alien race growing on any planet in a galaxy, at any level, the Seeders would just go around that galaxy.

Over the centuries, Seeder research ships would watch the alien development, but never interfere. It was one of their most scared laws, learned out of bad experience a long, long time ago.

Very few alien races even survived long enough to make it off their own planet. And even fewer found trans-tunnel drive to jump to other close stars. And for as long as humans had been seeding galaxies with more humans, no alien race had found the refinements to trans-tunnel drives to get the standard speeds to break out of their own limited galaxies.

Yet somehow, he was looking at an alien ship that was between galaxies.

And moving at standard trans-tunnel drive speeds.

"Any life signs at all of any type?" Tacita asked.

"Nothing," Commander Chain said. "We also checked for any form of stasis. Nothing."

Chain was their most trusted second in command on any ship and had been with them thousands of years. He looked, as most Seeders looked, to be about thirty. He had dark brown hair and never was seen out of jeans and a sweatshirt.

"How large is that ship?" Ray asked.

"The size of a Seeder mother ship," Chain said.

Seeder mother ships were the largest ships Seeder's built. Mother ships were the size of small moons and shaped like birds gliding. They could hold a thousand other ships and upwards of a million people comfortably.

"Any equipment at all active?" Tacita asked.

"Except for the trans-tunnel drive still powering it forward," Chain said. "Nothing is active. No atmosphere of any kind, no readings other than the drive. And honestly, it looks like the drive is about to fail as well."

"Can you get a reading on the age?" Ray asked.

"At least two hundred thousand standard years," Chase said. "And from the looks of the damage from impacts of small particles and such after its shields failed, it has been dead for a good hundred thousand of those years."

"Trace back its flight path and put up on the screen where it came from," Tacita said.

Ray was surprised when the image appeared of a thousand galaxies in all their various groupings. Right now they were in the middle of what was called the "Local Cluster" by humans in this galaxy. About thirty galaxies of different sizes and shapes. On the scale on the map on the screen, the local cluster barely showed up as a dot.

The alien ship had originated, or passed through a galaxy that was a vast distance away. Ray guessed there were four hundred galaxies between where it started and where it was now.

"I've accounted for galactic movement on the rough track," Chase said. "That ship never got near another galaxy of any size since it left that galaxy."

"At its speed," Ray asked, "was the ship still functioning when it left that galaxy?"

"Yes," Chase said. "From what we can gather on preliminary scans, it appears it left that galaxy very much alive and functioning."

A dot appeared about halfway along the line of travel on the big screen. "The ship went dead about at this point, from what we can tell so far."

"We need a massive amount of study of this ship," Tacita said. "To find out who this race was and what happened to this ship."

She looked at Ray and he nodded.

Ray agreed completely. They did need a massive amount of

study on this ship. And they were going to have to do it carefully and not miss anything.

But his eye went back along the line the ship had taken from that original galaxy. They also needed to know what was happening there and in the galaxies around it.

Two hundred thousand years had passed. Were these aliens expanding as humans did?

And were they warlike?

In space where very, very few advanced civilizations ever emerged from planets, what would the aliens even think if they knew humans were here and spread over hundreds of thousands of galaxies in this area?

Ray kept staring at the image of the ship's path on the wall screen.

Even by the galaxy-spanning scale Seeders worked and thought at, the alien original galaxy was a very, very long distance away.

NEWSLETTER SIGN-UP

Follow Dean on BookBub

Be the first to know!

Just sign up for the Dean Wesley Smith newsletter, and keep up with the latest news, releases and so much more—even the occasional giveaway.
So, what are you waiting for? To sign up go to deanwesleysmith.com.

But wait! There's more. Sign up for the WMG Publishing newsletter, too, and get the latest news and releases from all of the WMG authors and lines, including Kristine Kathryn Rusch, Kristine Grayson, Kris Nelscott, *Pulphouse Fiction Magazine*, *Smith's Monthly*, and so much more.
To sign up go to wmgpublishing.com.

ABOUT THE AUTHOR

Considered one of the most prolific writers working in modern fiction, *USA Today* bestselling writer Dean Wesley Smith published far more than a hundred novels in forty years, and hundreds of short stories across many genres.

At the moment he produces novels in several major series, including the time travel Thunder Mountain novels set in the Old West, the galaxy-spanning Seeders Universe series, the urban fantasy Ghost of a Chance series, a superhero series starring Poker Boy, and a mystery series featuring the retired detectives of the Cold Poker Gang.

His monthly magazine, *Smith's Monthly*, which consists of only his own fiction, premiered in October 2013 and offers readers more than 70,000 words per issue, including a new and original novel every month.

During his career, Dean also wrote a couple dozen *Star Trek* novels, the only two original *Men in Black* novels, Spider-Man and X-Men novels, plus novels set in gaming and television worlds. Writing with his wife Kristine Kathryn Rusch under the name Kathryn Wesley, he wrote the novel for the NBC miniseries The Tenth Kingdom and other books for *Hallmark Hall of Fame* movies.

He wrote novels under dozens of pen names in the worlds of comic books and movies, including novelizations of almost a dozen films, from *The Final Fantasy* to *Steel* to *Rundown*.

Dean also worked as a fiction editor off and on, starting at Pulphouse Publishing, then at *VB Tech Journal*, then Pocket Books, and now at WMG Publishing, where he and Kristine Kathryn Rusch serve as series editors for the acclaimed *Fiction River* anthology series.

For more information about Dean's books and ongoing projects, please visit his website at www.deanwesleysmith.com and sign up for his newsletter.

For more information:
www.deanwesleysmith.com

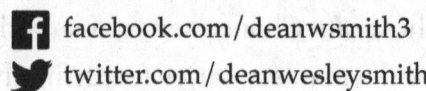 facebook.com/deanwsmith3
twitter.com/deanwesleysmith

www.ingramcontent.com/pod-product-compliance
Lightning Source LLC
Chambersburg PA
CBHW010734100726
47899CB00009B/3050